"Your face was very revealing, Lisa."

Before she could answer, Matt went on speaking. "When I interrupted your kiss with Peter that night, I had a perfect opportunity to judge what effect his lovemaking had on you," he continued. "Some things can't be hidden, especially from someone who's been around as much as I have...."

"I'm sure you're very experienced," Lisa retorted. "Why should you care, anyway?"

"I hate waste. You'd be throwing yourself away if you married that milk-and-water fellow!"

His hands reached out to pull her toward him. She was too startled to resist as his ruthless mouth fastened on her lips, parting them forcefully. Lisa had never before felt such a sensual onslaught. Opening her eyes, she drew a parched breath.

"There," he said huskily. "Now tell me Peter's kiss felt anything like that!"

Other titles by

CHARLOTTE LAMB
IN HARLEQUIN PRESENTS

Other titles by

CHARLOTTE LAMB
IN HARLEQUIN ROMANCES

CHARLOTTE LAMB

the cruel flame

Harlequin Books

TORONTO • LONDON • LOS ANGELES • AMSTERDAM
SYDNEY • HAMBURG • PARIS • STOCKHOLM • ATHENS • TOKYO

Harlequin Presents edition published October 1980
ISBN 0-373-10387-5

Original hardcover edition published in 1978
by Mills & Boon Limited

CHAPTER ONE

'STORM DANCE has been sold,' said Fran Baynard, bursting into the warm kitchen of her home suddenly, bringing the crisp, cold freshness of the autumn afternoon with her. Her cheeks were stinging with bright colour, her eyes shone. Small, slight, with curly fair hair and green eyes, she worked for the local newspaper and often brought home titbits of local gossip long before the grapevine had got hold of them.

Her elder sister, Lisa, straightened from the long black range from which she was extracting a beautifully browned sugar-dusted fruit cake. 'Storm Dance? Good lord! I thought the old place would fall down before someone actually bought it.'

'It's in a pretty bad state of repair,' Fran agreed, snatching a small hot currant cake and nibbling around the edges with her sharp white teeth.

'Don't touch them! They're for the bazaar tomorrow,' Lisa told her.

'Mmm ... they're very good. You never make cakes like this for us!'

'How often are you in for tea?' Lisa demanded, removing the currant cakes to a place of safety. 'So who has bought Storm Dance?'

'Oh, yes ...' Fran's eyes shone at her excitedly, her

cheeks deepening to a brighter pink. 'You'll never guess!'

'I'm not even going to try,' Lisa calmly told her. 'You're going to tell me, and you'd better hurry, because Peter will be here any minute, to drive these cakes to Mrs Evans for safe keeping. I don't dare leave them around here. If you don't get them, Timmy will.'

'Beast! I've a good mind not to tell you now.'

'You'll burst if you don't, so hurry up!' Lisa carefully, deftly, with amazing speed, packed the cakes into a round tin box.

Fran perched on the edge of the long deal table and watched her. 'I'll give you some clues ... who's the star of a tough police series, an ex-racing car champion and was born ten miles from here?'

Lisa's long, slim fingers halted in their task. She stared down at the cakes for a moment, then looked up, her rich chestnut hair falling back from her flushed face. 'Matt Wolfe?'

'Got it in one ... exciting, isn't it? Our local wonder boy returns home. According to Mr Prentice he was born in one of the cottages down by Pelly Bridge ... fantastic to think of it! Those places are fit only for rats....'

'They must have suited him, then.' Lisa finished packing the cakes and jammed the lid on the tin with unnecessary force. She turned away to get another tin into which she placed the fruit cake. Fran stared at her averted face, catching only a glimpse of one golden-brown eye and a long, straight nose.

'You don't like him, do you? You're in a minority, then. All the girls at school used to swoon over him.'

'The only TV star I swoon over is Snoopy,' Lisa said lightly. 'I detest tough police films. All that violence makes me sick.'

'Do you know what, you're a Victorian,' Fran told her. 'You should be sewing samplers and reading psalms all day.'

'I've got too much to do,' Lisa informed her tartly. 'If someone helped with the washing up I might get time to change before Peter gets here.'

'Bully!' Fran grimaced at her. 'All right, I'll do it. Though why you bother I can't imagine, because Peter Farrell has never noticed what you were wearing before! He isn't likely to start now.'

'Don't quarrel with him when he gets here!' Lisa commanded. 'You two never seem to see eye to eye. Try to be nice to him.'

'Just to please you I'll force myself not to offer him strychnine sandwiches or put arsenic into his coffee instead of sugar,' said Fran, turning towards the sink with a sigh.

Lisa laughed and went upstairs to change. As she slid into a smooth green woollen dress, her eye fell on a dark outline on the cliffs above her home. Storm Dance was more like a natural landmark than a house. Built in the nineteenth century by a sea captain who had made a fortune in some nefarious manner in the South Seas, it had been intended as much as a fortress as a home, the stone walls massively defiant, blending into their surroundings as if they had grown up out of the ground instead of being placed there by the hand of man. The name the sea captain gave the house had caused much local comment, but over the years it had come to seem the inevitable name for such a place. On stormy days the house stood out against the dark sky, like a granite monolith, defying the worst that wind and waves could throw at it.

It was, Lisa thought wryly, a very suitable place for Matt Wolfe to want to live in—his character would blend in perfectly with the house.

She sat down in front of the dressing-table and began to apply make-up rapidly. She had an oval face, her skin a creamy pink which health and vitality underlined. Her eyes were a warm golden-brown, the brown lashes surrounding them tipped with glinting gold. Her chestnut hair hung in loose waves to her shoulders. Tall, slim, energetic and capable, Lisa occasionally wished she was as slight and fragile as her younger sister. It was not always an asset to be as strong as a horse, although if you were a doctor's daughter and worked in the dual role of housekeeper and receptionist, health was certainly a necessity. Lisa's day began at six-thirty, when she got up and started the range to warm the kitchen. When she had prepared breakfast she called her father, sister and brother. While they ate, she went through to the surgery and made sure that her father's office was in order, checked all the appointments for that morning, got out the required cards and put them in order on her father's desk, switched on the central heating, checked on the waiting-room and then hurried back to the house to eat her own breakfast. While the others left for their various jobs, she washed up and began the preparations for lunch. Then she went through to the surgery again to open the door to the first patient. After surgery, she went back to the kitchen and finished preparing lunch. While her father did his rounds she was doing house-work.

After lunch she washed up again, then went back to the surgery to type out the letters her father wished to send. All the clerical work done, she went back to the house to prepare supper.

It was a long, hard day. Looking at herself critically, she thought: just as well I thrive on hard work! Fran could never stand up to the gruelling pace of life as Lisa knew it. Even as a child, Fran had been delicate. At school she had had a tendency to show signs of strain during examination periods, and Lisa had learnt to watch her closely for the telltale signs.

Their mother had died when Lisa was seventeen, and it had been obvious that Lisa must take over running the house. Fran was still at school, a pale, leggy schoolgirl of thirteen. Timmy was just ten, a freckled schoolboy with a shock of ginger hair and a pocketful of marbles. Doctor Baynard had been numb with shock for the first few months after his wife's death. When he came out of his grief he had suggested that he get help for Lisa, a housekeeper to take over from her, but Lisa had seen the horror in Fran's and Timmy's eyes at the idea, and she had shaken her head, insisting that she enjoyed running the house. It was true, even though she found herself stretched to the limit. The challenge of the job made her grow up fast. It had helped her over her own grief and given her face a new maturity overnight.

During that period her father had had a nurse/receptionist working for him in the surgery. Two years ago, this capable lady had given in her notice because her husband was being transferred to another job in Birmingham. Doctor Baynard advertised for a successor, but the applicants were not suitable, and Lisa had offered to work for him temporarily while he looked for someone else. Somehow, the job had become a permanent one. Her father gradually ceased to look for anyone else and Lisa gradually realised that she now had two jobs instead of one. By getting up an hour earlier, she managed to fit all the work into her busy day, but sometimes she wondered how she did it. Like most busy people, the more she did the more she found she could do. Time stretched to accommodate all she had to do.

'You're mad,' Peter Farrell sometimes told her. 'What does your father pay you? Peanuts! Look at your clothes! Jeans, old tweed skirts and sweaters ... how many really nice things do you have?'

'I could hardly do housework in a silk dress!' she had smiled at him. 'When would I get the chance to wear all these fine clothes you want me to buy?'

'When I take you out,' he had said flatly.

She had shaken her head at him with amusement. 'What? To the local art exhibition? Or to watch the amateur dramatic group doing *The Importance of Being Earnest* for the fourth time?'

'There's the dance at the town hall next week,' he had said seriously. 'What are you going to wear for that?'

'My green dress,' she had shrugged.

'You always wear the damned thing,' Peter had said angrily. 'I'm sick of the sight of it even if you aren't!'

She had laughed. 'Oh, poor Peter! Why didn't you tell me? I'll see what I can do!'

He had sighed then, his expression anxious. 'You're the Cinderella of your family. You ought to stand up for your rights more. Fran always has pretty clothes. Why shouldn't you? Your father can afford it.'

'Dad is very generous. If he thought I wanted a new dress he'd buy it for me at once. You misjudge him.' She had looked at him seriously. 'You don't understand how it is, Peter. We're so busy, Dad and I. We have no time to think about things like clothes. My day is jam-packed with jobs to do. When am I supposed to find time for shopping, let alone thinking about clothes?'

'You should make time,' he had said, his tone faintly sulky. 'When I take you out I like you to look good.'

She had gone into town on the following Saturday and bought herself a new dress to wear at the town hall dance, but she did nothing about the rest of her wardrobe. Her life was too full to leave room for personal vanity. She knew that her father's patients were far too wrapped up in their own problems to notice her appearance. So long as she was neat and well-groomed, her father barely noticed her either. Peter's views were pushed to the back of her mind and forgotten.

Now, staring at herself absently, she remembered them briefly. Her dress was two years old, a nicely cut classic style, well washed and pressed but still retaining a certain attraction. Peter had liked it when she first bought it, but she knew that he would look at it with resignation when they met. I really must try to find time to buy some more clothes, she told herself, but when she mentally scanned the weeks ahead she could not think of a day when she would be free to spend time on such a project.

Back in the kitchen she found Fran putting away the washed cake tins while Peter leaned against the wall, watching her silently, his expression wintry. Peter and Fran did not like each other. Peter disapproved of Fran because she left so much of the day-to-day running of the house to Lisa, and Fran disliked Peter because she thought him supercilious and critical. The atmosphere between them now could be cut with a knife.

'I'm ready,' said Lisa, moving into the room.

Peter glanced at her, sighed as his eye ran over her and said, 'So I see.'

'You sound as enthusiastic as an Eskimo offered an ice lolly,' Fran said tartly.

'Perhaps if your sister had time to get out of this

house once in a while and buy herself some new clothes, I would feel more enthusiasm,' Peter snapped.

'Lisa is at home all day. She could drive into town any time she liked!' Fran retorted.

'How is she supposed to do that? She never has a second to herself. Even now, we're only delivering these damned cakes, not going out to enjoy ourselves,' Peter said angrily.

'How sad!' Fran moved to the door, her honey-blonde curls dancing on her shoulders. 'I must find a hankie before I burst into tears.'

Peter glared after her. 'Butterfly brain! That girl is so selfish I could slap her.'

'She's very young,' Lisa said indulgently.

'For heaven's sake! When you were three years younger than Fran you were running this house!'

'Yes, but Fran is delicate,' Lisa excused.

'Delicate my eye! That girl is as delicate as King Kong. You just spoil her, you and your father. You let her get away with everything. How many nights a week do you get out? I'll tell you—one or two at most. How often does Fran get out? Every single damned night. And a different boy every time. She gets through boy-friends the way most women get through paper tissues.'

'Oh, Peter, don't pick a quarrel with me over Fran! You always seem to be so quarrelsome lately. What's the matter with you?' Lisa looked at him with anxious concern, her golden-brown eyes wide.

He sighed, moving closer to her, and took her by

the shoulders, looking down into her upturned face with a frown which made thin lines across his forehead. When he was old, she thought suddenly, he would have dozens of lines in his face from frowning.

'I'm frustrated, I suppose,' Peter said. 'We've been seeing each other for years, but we never seem to get anywhere. Your family block every road. They're always around, demanding your attention. I can never get close to you.'

'You're close enough, now,' she murmured with a teasing little smile, linking her arms around his neck.

For a moment he resisted her warmth, then he laughed reluctantly, bending towards her. They kissed gently, leaning against each other, without passion or excitement. Lisa wondered for a moment if this was how love really was, not the dazzling explosion one read about in books, but a quiet fondness and familiarity. Was it enough? she thought, and pushed the question away into the treacherous recesses of her mind.

After a moment Peter drew away and she smiled up at him. 'I hate to say this, but we really have to go. If I don't get these cakes to Mrs Evans she'll complain bitterly.' She grinned at him apologetically. 'Don't hit the roof, darling.'

Peter groaned. 'Why do I put up with it? Oh, lead on, Macduff. I'll bring the cake tins.'

When they had delivered the cakes Peter asked her if there was anything else he could do for her. He meant it as a piece of irony, but she took it seriously.

'I've got some shopping to do,' she said. 'Could you drop me in the town?'

'I suppose so,' he said sulkily.

'Is it taking you out of your way?' she asked, looking at him with a sigh.

'I'd hoped we could have some time to ourselves,' he told her, scowling.

'If you come round tonight we could watch television together,' she suggested.

'What a thrill!' His voice was sarcastic. 'With your father and Timmy to keep us company, I suppose?'

She sighed. 'I doubt it. Timmy will be doing his homework and Dad rarely watches television, you know.'

'And Fran, of course, will be out with one of her boy-friends,' Peter snapped. 'As usual.'

He drove along the steep road down into Saintpel without saying anything much. Lisa leaned back, watching the view with her usual feeling of warm pleasure.

Saintpel was a small Cornish fishing town with a few thousand inhabitants, six churches, a few dozen public houses and a rocky bay in which many ships had been wrecked over the centuries until the lighthouse was built in the nineteenth century to warn against the danger of needle-sharp rocks beneath the great grey waves which rolled in across the bay.

In high summer tourists flooded into the little town to exclaim over the quaintness of the narrow streets, the beach and cliffs, the rockpools with their marine inhabitants. But once summer was over Saintpel returned to its ancient peace, a peace much cherished by the older inhabitants, but resented by the younger ones who longed for bright lights and gay evenings.

There was nothing much to do in Saintpel after dark in winter. Everything shut promptly at five-thirty. The shopping street was deserted. The only places open were the pubs, and they were always throbbing with life. In consequence the local people made much of their own entertainment. Amateur dramatics, amateur music, art classes and adult education thrived. The tiny cinema only opened two evenings a week and ran on an amateur basis, subsidised by the local council. Television and radio were desperately important to those whose social lives were so limited.

Fran had often said to Lisa that she felt she was someone in an Edgar Allan Poe story who had been buried alive. 'One day I'll burn the town down,' she would threaten half seriously. 'The place is moribund, totally moribund.'

'People come to visit Saintpel from all parts of the globe,' Lisa sometimes reminded her. 'It's a famous beauty spot.'

'They can have it!' Fran would say, hunching an irritable shoulder.

Staring down at the steel-grey sea Lisa remembered what Fran had told her about Storm Dance. It would cause a sensation in the town to have a TV star living in the old house. Why on earth was he doing it?

Had he forgotten what a grim place Saintpel could

be in winter? He ought to know. He had been born just ten miles away in a tiny hamlet surrounding the bridge over the Pelly river. The haphazard, tumbledown cottages still stood as they had for several centuries, grey stone walls furred with damp green moss, dark slate roofs, warped and sagging windows, cramped little rooms with sloping ceilings and woodworm in the floorboards, if gossip spoke the truth.

It was an unlikely place for a television star to spring from, she thought drily.

Matt Wolfe had first sprung to the public's attention when he was twenty-one and began racing cars in a small way. He had progressed rapidly, winning his races in a daring, spectacular fashion which caught the mind of the public. By the time he was twenty-four he was famous. His tough good looks brought him lots of publicity and his skill at the wheel made him popular with his audience.

It must have been when he was around twenty-five that he had a really serious crash while racing in France. In the same accident his best friend, a small, dark Welshman, had been killed. The story had made headlines everywhere. Matt Wolfe suffered serious injuries which kept him out of racing for six months. He recovered, although he had had a scar above his left eye ever since, but he had not returned to the race track.

Instead he had become a stunt driver for films. Within a very short time he had been given a few bit parts to play. He had a darkly handsome face which proved excessively photogenic. After several small parts he got a part in a television series, a small supporting role as a police detective.

For some reason the series quickly shot to the top of the ratings and he became a household name. Over the last three years the part had been built up until now he was the star of the series. Tough, aggressive, intensely masculine, he acted everyone else off the screen. When he was around he dominated every second of the time.

Sex appeal, Lisa thought drily. That was what he had, presumably. She had never been able to see it, herself. The series was filled with the sort of violence which made her sick. Whenever she had seen it she had felt a quiver of antipathy towards him, although, if she were honest, she knew nothing against him except the part he played, and as he was an actor it was unfair to judge by that. She suspected, from what she knew of his private life, however, that his real character was not so far removed from the role he played.

The car lurched down into Saintpel High Street and slowed to a crawl.

'Where shall I drop you?' Peter asked her.

'Anywhere you like,' she said. 'I've got a number of things to buy.'

'Not clothes, I suppose?' he said wearily.

'I might look for a new dress if I've got time,' she said in wary apology.

Peter stopped the car outside the butcher's shop, and she climbed out, giving him a wave as she turned away. She spent a few minutes discussing the weather with the butcher, then chose some lamb chops and a couple of oxtails. This was definitely the weather for oxtail stew, she thought, walking briskly towards the greengrocer's.

The shops were already closing up. She hurried through the rest of her shopping and turned back towards the far end of town to face the long walk home. If she was lucky the bus would be running late. It sometimes did, and then she would catch it instead of having to walk home. The next bus was at seven-thirty. There was no point in waiting for that.

Passing the estate agent's office she met Tony Wyman, Fran's latest boy-friend, shuffling about on the pavement, one eye on his watch, his shoulders hunched against the autumn wind.

'Waiting for Fran?' she asked him with a smile.

He shook his head. 'Matt Wolfe,' he said, with some relish, watching her to see her response.

So that was where Fran had got her information! Lisa thought, with amusement.

'Taking him up to view Storm Dance?' she asked.

He looked crestfallen. 'How did you know?'

'Fran told me,' she said.

'Oh, of course,' Tony nodded.

She looked round in dismay as she saw the small red bus beginning to throb and quiver preparatory to starting off on its journey up the cliff road and over the green fields to the next town. 'Oh, I'll miss it,' she groaned, leaping out into the road.

There was a grinding of brakes and a long, red sports car swerved violently to avoid her. Going pale, she leapt back onto the pavement. The driver of the sports car stopped dead, backed and climbed out to confront her.

Looking a long way up at him she recognised Matt Wolfe, and the shock she had just received made that recognition unreal. His face was so familiar, yet somehow strange.

He was taller than he seemed on television, his lean frame making his height deceptive. The dark hair was windblown into a fashionably wild look. The very bright blue eyes were angry, the scar over the left one giving him a distinctly piratical air which somehow increased the threat he emanated as he towered over her.

'What the hell do you think you're doing? Do you realise I nearly killed you? You stepped off the pavement without looking, right under my wheels. If I wasn't a damned good driver I'd have left you in a dozen assorted bits!'

Lisa's feeling of guilty self-reproach dissolved under his tongue lashing. She felt her spine tingle with antagonism. Admittedly she was at fault, but he had no right to shout at her in the street like that, menacing her in that dangerous fashion.

Her golden-brown eyes were suddenly stormy as she glared back at him. 'You were driving too fast. We don't expect lunatics to come down Saintpel High Street at eighty miles an hour!'

'I was doing fifty,' he said between his teeth. 'Have you ever driven a car, young woman? If you have, you should know that drivers depend on people doing the sensible thing, which in this case means looking before they step into the road!'

The slow roar of the bus caught her attention. She stared after it as it drew away from the bus stop. 'Now I've missed it!' she said furiously. 'I'll have to walk two miles up Saintpel Cliff, thanks to you!'

'At least you'll get there in one piece,' he said disagreeably. 'If I don't throttle you first, that is. . . .'

She turned away, her head held high, and began to walk down the road. Her shopping basket was heavy and her spirits sagged at the thought of that long, windy walk home.

Behind her she heard Tony saying nervously, 'Mr Wolfe? I'm Tony Wyman. We spoke on the telephone. . . .' She sympathised with the slight shake in his young voice. Who wouldn't be nervous confronted with six foot-odd of masculine aggression cloaked in sardonic authority?

Matt Wolfe didn't answer, and she discovered why when she felt his hand on her arm. Turning, bristling at once, ready for a further argument, she was astounded to hear him say brusquely, 'I'll drive you home. Get in the car.'

She almost refused, her mood defiant, but something in the way he was regarding her made her think better of it. She would have done almost anything to avoid that long walk home, anyway.

He opened the door of his car and gestured. 'Get in. . . .'

When she was seated he turned to Tony. 'I'll be back in ten minutes.' He glanced across the road at the pub sign swinging in the wind. 'It's cold out here. Wait in there, I'll buy you a drink before we go up to Storm Dance.'

Tony's face was sulky as he nodded, but he made no protest. He needed that sale too much, Lisa thought in sudden wry amusement.

Matt Wolfe climbed into the driver's seat, clipping on his seat belt immediately. He glanced at her and ordered, 'Do your belt up, for God's sake, woman!'

'They make me feel claustrophobic,' she explained.

'In my car you wear a seat belt,' he directed tightly.

'Insurance reasons?' she guessed.

'Do it up and don't argue,' he snapped. The blue eyes watched smoulderingly as she clipped the belt, then he started the car. The engine gave a dramatic roar and they shot away.

She watched appreciatively as he drove, unable to avoid admiring the way the long, capable fingers handled the instruments. The car was expensive, luxurious, comfortable. They soon began to eat up the distance, passing the bus like the wind as it lumbered along, puffing and panting.

He gave her an arrogant tight-lipped smile. 'You'll be home before the bus,' he said.

She stared at the livid scar above his dark eyebrow, the fleshless angle of the cheekbone, the jut of the strong chin. He was a man you would find it hard to forget.

'What's your name?' he asked casually, turning his attention back to the road.

'Lisa Baynard,' she said.

At once his eyes grinned round at her ironically. 'Sounds like a stage name.'

'Well, it isn't,' she said.

'Where exactly do you live?' he asked. 'I know this area quite well.' She explained quickly and he nodded. 'I know the house. Doctor's house, isn't it?'

'My father,' she said.

He glanced at her again. 'Girl of few words, aren't you? Except when you're angry.'

She flushed, her creamy skin filling with colour, her eyes as dangerously bright as fireworks. His eyes narrowed with a sudden gleam.

'So what do you do with yourself in Saintpel, Lisa Baynard? Apart from stepping under cars?'

'I work for my father,' she said coldly.

'Receptionist?'

'Among other things.'

'Does it keep you busy?'

She smiled a little grimly. 'Yes,' she said.

'Do you know Storm Dance?' he asked, after a brief pause. 'The house up on the cliffs there....'

'I know it,' she said, looking along the cliffs at the stone walls defiantly facing into the wind. There were few trees around the house. Nothing but low shrubs could survive the onslaught of that salt-drenched gale.

A few thorn trees survived, twisted into barbaric shapes, their branches shaped by the prevailing wind. They had a tattered air of obstinacy, as though determined to cling to their ground whatever the elements flung at them. Lisa had always felt an odd sympathy for them. She admired their tenacity.

'Aren't you going to get bored living up there?' she asked him, her tone unconsciously contemptuous.

He looked at her again with that narrowed, dangerous glance. 'If I thought that I wouldn't buy it.'

'I would have thought you would prefer a house nearer London,' she said. 'You'll have to be there quite a bit, won't you?'

'I've just finished the new series of *The Squad*, so I'm free for a few months. I'll have time to settle in before I go to America in the spring to make a film.'

'What's the film going to be about?'

'Racing,' he said, tersely.

'Motor racing?'

'Yes.' The monosyllable was irritable.

He drew up outside her house and turned to stare at her lazily. 'Got a date tonight?'

'Yes,' she said, too quickly.

His brows arched mockingly. 'Why so nervous?'

'I'm not,' she snapped, reaching for the door handle. She couldn't work out how it operated, and he reached across her to do it, his lean face inches away from hers. She pressed back in her seat to avoid him and the blue eyes swerved to look at her penetratingly.

'I'm not about to make a pass,' he drawled. 'No need for your pulses to flutter.'

She stared back at him, her face icy. 'My pulses will never flutter for you,' she said scornfully.

He laughed, blue eyes dancing. 'Famous last words!'

'My God,' she said, disgusted. 'You ought to buy a suitcase to carry your ego around in ... the weight must be killing you!'

His laughter rose again, untouched by her sarcasm. She slid out of the car and walked up the path without a backward glance, passing Fran, who was coming out.

As Lisa paused to open the front door she heard Matt Wolfe say coolly, 'Are you going into Saintpel? Want a lift?'

She turned to watch as Fran practised her fluttering eyelashes on him and smiled sweetly. 'Thank you. That's very kind of you.'

Lisa suddenly guessed that her sister had seen the car arrive and recognised the driver. Fran was far too unsurprised. She must have had time to think out a plan of campaign before she came sauntering down the garden path at that precise moment in such an opportune fashion.

Matt Wolfe swung his passenger door open again and Fran climbed into the seat beside him. He leaned past her to shut the door. His bright, mocking blue eyes met Lisa's deliberately.

She turned away and went into the house. Fran was old enough to look after herself. If she chose to scrape acquaintance with him that was her business.

Later that evening Lisa and Peter sat in the kitchen, listening to the slow heartbeat of the grandfather clock in the hall, and the soft sighing of the ash falling through the grate in the range. Doctor Baynard was in bed hours ago and probably asleep by now. Timmy, too, was in bed. Normally Lisa would have turned in herself, but Peter seemed determined to force an argument with her, and she was forced to stay up to placate him.

'What do you expect me to do? How long am I to hang around waiting for you to marry me?' he asked her. 'Take a good long look at yourself. You're turning into an old woman before you're twenty-five. Your hair is unfashionable, your clothes are worse and you've no spring in your step. You hurry from job to job, hardly stopping to take stock of where you're going.'

'I'll promise to do something about my clothes,' she said, smiling at him. 'I'll speak to Dad tomorrow.'

'I hope you will,' said Peter. He picked up her hand and kissed it softly. 'Oh, I'm sorry if I've been nagging you again. I get so angry when I think of the waste ... we ought to be married with a home of our own by now.'

'Is this a proposal?' she asked lightly, laughing.

'I've been proposing to you for three years without much visible result,' Peter said.

Lisa moved nearer him on the old oak settle with its high back and gingham cushions. 'You'll have to go soon. It's nearly eleven and Fran should be back soon. Kiss me goodnight.'

'Now you're talking,' said Peter, sliding his arms around her. They kissed slowly, their arms around each other. Not for the first time Lisa wondered if it was normal for a woman to feel as she did when Peter kissed her. It was a pleasant experience, warming and friendly, but there was no emotional excitement in it. Was that an element only found in books? Was love always as cosy as an old slipper? Perhaps her own lack of urgency where Peter was concerned was because of a secret, underlying hesitation about committing herself to him for ever.

The back door was flung open suddenly, making them spring apart. Lisa stood up, her cheeks flushed, her rich chestnut hair ruffled and untidy. She was very slim and graceful in her green wool dress, the age of it concealed by this dim lighting.

'Lisa! I didn't expect you to be up at this time?' Fran stood in the doorway, her expression startled.

Lisa looked at the man behind her sister with a faint smile which vanished as she recognised him.

'Sorry if we interrupted anything,' Matt Wolfe drawled, strolling forward, his narrowed blue eyes flicking up and down over Lisa.

Peter stood up at that moment, rather pink, his brown hair as ruffled as Lisa's. 'I must be off,' he muttered, scowling at Fran and her companion. 'Goodnight, darling.'

'I'll see you to your car,' Lisa offered.

'Don't bother. It's cold outside,' he said, vanishing into the darkness.

'I'm afraid we arrived inopportunely,' Matt Wolfe said with a hint of mockery.

'Not at all,' she said defensively. 'I was just saying goodnight to him when you came in. . . .'

'Obviously,' he drawled, his glance resting on her smudged lipstick.

She put up a concealing hand to her mouth, then flushed deeper with irritation.

'Lisa, this is Matt Wolfe,' said Fran, triumph in her tone as she spoke.

'Obviously,' Lisa imitated sarcastically.

He laughed softly.

Lisa gave him a smouldering look of deep dislike. 'Goodnight, Fran,' she said. 'I'm off to bed. Don't stay down here too late.'

'I'm a big girl now,' Fran protested on a note of irritated indignation. 'I can run my own life without your help. Stop nagging!'

Lisa bit her lip and turned towards the door. Over her shoulder she said calmly, 'You do have to be up early, though. It isn't sensible to stay down here talking when you need your sleep.'

'Talking?' Fran giggled. 'Be your age, Lisa!'

Flushing, Lisa bit back a reproachful reply. Matt Wolfe moved gracefully past her and opened the door to allow her through. Aware of his brilliant blue gaze, she ignored him apart from a brief inclination of the head and a 'Thank you' delivered in icy tones.

'Pleasant dreams, Miss Baynard,' he murmured mockingly, closing the door behind her.

Rigid with dislike, she went upstairs and into the bathroom. Later, her face clean and glowing, her slim body wrapped in her shabby old blue dressing-gown, she was about to get into bed when she realised she had forgotten to get a hot water bottle. The sheets were icy. Shivering, she dived out of bed again and went downstairs to the kitchen. The house was totally silent. There were no lights to be seen anywhere and she was sure she had heard the front door close behind Matt Wolfe ten minutes ago.

But when she returned to the kitchen she opened the door to halt in her tracks, her expression shocked.

By the warm red glow from the range she saw her little sister in his arms being ruthlessly kissed, her slight body bent backwards over his arm, her hands clasped behind the back of his neck.

The gasp she gave distracted them from their embrace. Fran looked round angrily, flushing. 'For heaven's sake, Lisa, can't you leave us alone?'

Lisa was rooted to the spot, her own face scarlet. Matt Wolfe eyed her quizzically, his smile mocking. After a dreadful pause, Lisa turned and fled, pursued up the stairs by the memory of Matt Wolfe's amused, ironic eyes.

CHAPTER TWO

ONCE a week Lisa seized the opportunity to get out of the house alone, taking Robby, her cocker spaniel, for a long walk across the fields between Sunday breakfast and Sunday lunch. Leaving Timmy and Fran to do the washing-up while the roast slowly cooked, surrounded by golden roast potatoes, she would set out feeling like the battered survivor of a shipwreck, exhausted but eager.

The Sunday after Matt arrived in Saintpel, she decided to walk up towards Storm Dance for a last look at the house as it was now. Very soon, according to Fran, an army of builders would descend upon it and transform it. It had never been a beautiful house, but familiarity confers upon anything a sort of intimate beauty—even an ugly building can become beloved after years have passed. Lisa wanted to see Storm Dance once more as she had always known it—decaying, massive, stubbornly defiant. Judging by what she had heard of Matt Wolfe his taste, she thought, was likely to run to garish colour schemes and bogus antiquities. No doubt he would turn Storm Dance into a cosy nonentity.

When she and Robby set out the wind was blowing fiercely from the landside of Saintpel. They made rapid time over the climbing downland behind the cliffs, blown forward by the buffeting autumn wind. The fields had been ploughed recently. Rich brown earth lay in neat furrows, scattered with the powdery white of lime. A flock of seagulls rose, squawking, from the furrows as Robby ran at them, barking furiously.

A greenfinch hung delicately among the tangled twigs of a hedge, pecking at the last red berries. In the valley below the downs she could see a spiral of pale smoke wreathing up into the line of poplars which edged a wedge of farmland. The farmer's wife moved in the rambling garden beside the house, pegging out a few diapers on the washing line. The sky was the colour of smoke, too—misty, grey, touched with soft blue in places.

The landscape had that bare, stripped look of approaching winter. The colours were subdued, muted, gentle; greys and blues and whites thrown into relief by the brown of the ploughed earth and the stark dark lines of tree and hedge.

On such days Lisa loved to walk along the cliffs, with the stormy winter sea on one hand and the countryside on the other, her eyes turning constantly from one to the other.

Robby was in his element, plunging into the hedgerows with the optimism of his species, snuffling among fallen leaves in hope of starting a rabbit, his long ears twitching, his tail wagging in a ruffled plume of gold. As a puppy he had been small enough to sit in a teacup, his smooth golden head so innocent and tender that it had moved Lisa almost to tears. Now he was clumsy-footed, bouncing, a rascal in search of plunder on their walks, but with liquid eyes which could still beg their way out of trouble.

Storm Dance was shuttered and empty-looking as they approached it. An old tin pail clattered across the gravel, blown by the wind. Seagulls roosting on the roof stared bright-eyed across the sea watching the waves for signs of movement below.

Robby ran ahead, barking at an imaginary shadow. When Lisa came up behind him she was just in time to see his plumed tail vanish into the house. The front door swung open on its hinges, creaking.

'Robby! Here, boy!' she called, startled and alarmed.

His answering bark came from deep within the dark house. She stood at the door, calling again. There was a movement in the shadows within, then Matt Wolfe came out of the hall and stood, studying her coolly, his black head to one side.

'Well, well, well—the other Miss Baynard. What are you doing up here?'

Lisa was angry, at once; on the defensive in the face of what she saw as reproof.

'I often walk up here on a Sunday. I always have. Of course, when you've actually bought the house, I'll keep away, don't worry. While it was empty it didn't seem to matter. There was no one here to object.'

'Did I say I objected?' His hard mouth twisted in what might have been a smile. The blue eyes were sharp and cool.

She shrugged. 'I thought you were registering some sort of disapproval.'

'You're too quick in leaping to conclusions,' he replied. 'Come in.'

She glanced past him into the shadowy hall. 'No, thank you. I was just calling my dog. . . .'

'I suspect he's found a cosy fire to sit beside,' Matt Wolfe drawled.

She was surprised. 'Have you moved in already? That was quick.'

'I'm here for a few days to work out a scheme for the decorations,' he told her. 'I'm camping out in one room. The house is an icebox, so I lit a log fire and I've been hunched over it all morning, staring at books of wallpaper and paint charts, until I'm well near blind. Your dog came into the room and settled down beside the fire. I thought I was seeing things for a moment. You'd better come and get him yourself. He seems settled for the rest of the day.'

Reluctantly Lisa moved past him into the hall and walked through the darkness towards the faint orange glow which came from a back room.

When she looked into the room she was amused to find Robby, as she had been told, stretched out on a small hearthrug in front of a blazing log fire, his head on his paws, lazily content.

She laughed, and Matt Wolfe, at her elbow, made a small grunt of surprise.

Turning, she found him eyeing her with an enigmatic expression. 'So you can look human after all,' he told her.

She felt herself flush, and to cover her embarrassment looked round the shadowy room. It was a long, high-ceilinged drawing-room with a massive black marble fireplace which reminded her of a tombstone. The ceilings were ornamented with medallions in which gilded cherubs and sprays of flowers were displayed. Peeling wallpaper hung from the walls in dusty scrolls. In one corner was arranged a low camp bed covered by a thick scarlet blanket. Next to the fireplace stood a folding steel deck-chair with two cushions lying in it. Books of wallpaper, curtain patterns and paint cards were scattered on the floor.

On a small camp table stood a bottle of white wine, a glass and a plate of cheese and celery.

'I'm living on basic rations,' Matt Wolfe said, watching her.

'It looks very peaceful,' she murmured, her voice unconsciously wistful.

'Sit down and have a glass of wine,' he suggested.

'Oh, no! I couldn't!' Her horrified expression brought a wry smile to his lips.

'I'm offering you wine, not seduction,' he said tersely.

Her chin lifted defiantly. 'I didn't think. . . .'

'Oh yes, you did,' he interrupted.

'Nothing was further from my mind! I barely know you. Why should I suspect anything of the sort?'

'You have a revealing face,' he said. 'Your thoughts pass over it like the wind over a still pool.'

Her golden-brown eyes widened in perplexity. 'I

have to get back to cook Sunday lunch. That's why I refused your kind invitation.'

He stared down into her face, one brow quizzically arched. 'Your manners are excellent when you remember them.'

She looked away. 'I'm sorry if I sounded rude. But it is a long walk back to my house and my father hates meals to be late.'

'I've got my car in the stables round the back. I'll run you back home after you've had a drink.'

She hesitated, biting her lip. 'You're a very obstinate man, aren't you?'

He moved towards the table and poured wine into the glass. 'Sit down by the fire. Your dog has better instincts. He knows a good thing when he sees it.' He moved towards her as she hesitantly sank back against the cushions in the deck-chair. Bending over her, he put the glass into her hand, and his sudden nearness brought a curious wave of awareness. She became acutely uneasy, her fingers shaking as she clutched the wine.

He leaned against the broad marble mantelpiece. 'What do you think of the house?'

'I've always been very fond of it,' she admitted.

'Then you're just the person to advise me on the décor,' he returned calmly. 'This room, for instance ... what would you do with it?'

She looked round the room slowly. There was a mass of ivy tumbling over the windowsills outside as if trying to get in, a tangle of branches whipping about in the wind, blocking the light, so that the room looked dark and inhospitable.

'I'd clear the trees and ivy first,' she said thoughtfully. 'Then you'd be able to see the room better.' Her eyes touched on the hearth. 'And that fireplace ... it would look great on someone's tomb, but it looks ghastly in here.'

'I agree,' he nodded. 'I shall have something white and graceful put in its place. What about the ceiling?'

'I rather like that plasterwork,' she said, glancing up.

'And the walls?'

'You want something light and warm in here,' she said slowly.

He bent and selected a book of wallpapers, flicked over the pages and then held out the book to her. 'What about that?'

It was a pattern in a Regency style; white with apple-green stripes laced with a thin gold line. It was gay and spring-like. Lisa liked it instantly.

'That should look very good in here,' she agreed, surprised by his taste. She had expected him to like gaudier styles, somehow.

'With white woodwork?'

She nodded. 'It sounds marvellous.'

He looked at her glass. 'You aren't drinking your wine.'

She sipped it cautiously. He moved behind her again and after a moment she was astonished to hear the calm sanity of Bach behind her, the Brandenburg Concerto No. 2.

She glanced round, her rich chestnut hair against her windblown, flushed cheeks. Matt Wolfe was standing just at her shoulder, his hands in his pockets, listening to the music and watching her profile with a faintly brooding expression.

'That's how I want this room to look,' he said softly.

'Yes,' she said, understanding him. 'Have you got a record player here too?'

'A cassette player,' he shrugged. 'Battery powered. The electric power has been switched off. I've got a portable gas lamp and some candles. I could have an interior decorator to help me, but I want to do it all myself.' He paused, then moved past her to pick up a sketchbook. 'I've done some of the upstairs rooms.'

Lisa took the sketchbook and opened it, astonished by the charm of the drawings he had done of the rooms as he envisaged them. He had indicated the furnishings and colours with great skill.

'You're very good at this sort of thing,' she said.

'I wanted to be an artist when I was at school, but I got bitten by the racing bug instead.'

'Peter teaches art at our local comprehensive,' she told him.

He took the sketchbook out of her hands with an abrupt movement. 'Peter ... that's the chap I met briefly the other night. Sorry about the interruption. I hope I didn't spoil a big romantic moment.'

The unconcealed mockery in his tone made her lips tighten. 'Peter and I know each other too well for that.'

His brows arched mockingly. 'Too well for romance? How sad!'

Lisa flushed. 'Too well to have anything spoiled by an interruption, Mr Wolfe.'

'Matt,' he suggested. 'In my world we aren't accustomed to such formality.'

She glanced down at her half-finished wine. 'My world is very different from yours.'

'So I gather. I shall call you Lisa all the same. Otherwise I might confuse you with your sister, and that wouldn't do, would it?'

She wasn't sure what he meant. His tone held depths she preferred not to investigate. She stood up, placing her wine on the table. 'I must go, I'm afraid. I've still got to cook the vegetables.'

'What are you having for lunch? The usual Sunday meal, I suppose? Roast and all the trimmings?'

She nodded. 'Roast beef today. My father's favourite.'

'With horseradish sauce and Yorkshire pudding?' He looked at her pleadingly. 'I suppose you won't take pity on a stranded traveller? All I've got for lunch is cheese and celery.'

Faced with the question, she could hardly refuse. Politely she said, 'Of course. Do come. I'm sure my father will be very pleased to meet you.'

'Thank you,' he said gravely. A glint of humour in the blue eyes made her suspect that he was aware of her own reservations and amused by them.

She called Robby, who reluctantly stood up, yawning and stretching himself.

Carefully Matt Wolfe placed an old brass fireguard around the hearth, pushing the hearthrug back from the fire. His care surprised her. Catching her curious glance, he grimaced.

'I learnt caution in a hard school.' His finger flicked derisively at the scar above his eye. 'When my car crashed that last time I was trapped for five minutes. They only just got me out before the whole car went up in flames. I was lucky to get out alive. Another minute and I'd have been roasted alive.'

She shuddered. 'How terrible! No wonder you stopped racing.'

'That wasn't why I stopped,' he said tersely.

Her lips parted on a question, but she drew it back, biting her lower lip.

He grinned at her. 'I like that.'

'What?' She was puzzled.

'Tact in a woman. It's a rare gift. Most women ask questions in barefaced curiosity without realising how far they pry into private matters.'

They moved out of the house, pausing while he locked the door. Robby had rushed out, panting excitedly. Lisa whistled him back and he flew towards her, tail wagging, knocking her off her feet at his impact, his paws leaping up to her chest, his tongue happily hanging out of his grinning mouth.

Matt Wolfe caught her round the waist as she reeled backwards. His hard, muscled body supported her as she recovered her balance.

'Get down, you idiotic dog!' he commanded.

Robby obediently crouched, hangdog at once.

Lisa felt her pulses accelerating until she could hear them like jungle drums in her head. She straightened away from him, but his hand still curved round her waist below the sharp uplift of her breasts. She could feel the warmth of those strong, slim fingers even through her yellow sweater.

They were so close she could see the lividity of his scar, the whiteness edging his blue eyes, the thick dark lashes half lowered as he looked down at her.

'All right now?' he asked softly.

'Yes, thank you,' she said, trying to control the shaking which was creeping over her body.

'Your eyes remind me of a lion's eyes,' he said in that strange, soft tone. 'The rest of you is gentle and domestic, but you have the pagan eyes of a wild animal. It's a strange contrast.'

She tried to laugh. 'You have a vivid imagination!'

His mouth twisted mockingly. 'Far more vivid than you suspect,' he drawled.

She slid away from him, aware of flushed face and wide, nervous eyes. 'We really must hurry or lunch will be ruined.'

He followed her round towards the stables, his feet crunching on the gravel path.

His red car was parked in one of the old stable buildings. Old withered straw still blew about on the cobbled yard. Some sparrows had built a nest in the eaves below the old clock tower, the clock of which still stood at half past twelve. A battered iron weathercock blew restlessly to and fro, pointing east.

'Do you ride?' he asked her as he opened the passenger door for her.

'I did when I was at school. Father used to do his rounds on a horse when I was little, but of course as the practice grew he had to stop.'

'I shall have some horses when the house is ready for occupation,' he told her. 'You must come up and exercise them with me.'

'Fran loves horses, too,' she said quietly.

He laid his long hands on the steering wheel and stared up at the sky. 'Is that a hint?'

She flushed again. 'I thought....'

'I kissed your sister once, the kiss you saw. It was a gesture expected of me after our pleasant evening together, no more.' He turned and faced her, sitting sideways. 'Don't pair me off with your sister, Lisa. I don't like cages.'

'What happens between you and Fran is your business,' she said stiffly.

'Nothing is going to happen between myself and your sister,' he said harshly. 'Get that into your head.'

She looked down at her hands. Robby, on the back seat, was sitting up staring out of the window, panting.

After a long moment of silence, Matt started the car and drove out of the garage.

'Is your relationship with the art teacher official?' he asked coolly, staring ahead as he drove down the windy, exposed cliff road.

'We aren't engaged, if that's what you mean.'

'You know what I mean,' he said crisply. 'Has he asked you to marry him?'

'Many times,' she said.

'Yet you aren't engaged? Why not?'

'I have other people to consider. My father, Timmy, Fran.'

'Something could always be arranged if you really decided to get married,' he said.

'It's very difficult.'

'It's nothing of the kind. If you loved the man you'd find a way through the difficulties.'

Lisa was quiet.

'Do you?' he demanded.

She looked up. 'Do I what?'

His mouth twisted as he met her eyes briefly. 'Do you love him? You knew what I was asking.'

Her face was pink. 'You have no right to ask me that!'

'I suspect you don't love him,' he went on, as if she had not spoken. 'Otherwise you'd be married by now.'

'You barely know me. How can you possibly set up as a judge of my feelings?'

He braked abruptly and turned towards her, his face dark with some sudden emotion.

Lisa shrank away, startled.

'There are some things one can tell from a single look,' he said tightly. 'I told you that your face was very revealing. When we came in that night and interrupted your kiss, I had a perfect opportunity to judge what sort of effect his lovemaking had on you. Some things can't be hidden, especially from someone who's been around as much as I have....'

'I'm sure you're very experienced,' she said furiously. 'But I'm not an actress.'

'That's precisely why your face reveals so much!'

'What business is it of yours? It's nothing to do with you!'

'I hate waste,' he bit out savagely. 'You'd be throwing yourself away if you married that milk-and-water fellow!'

'Peter isn't milk-and-water!'

'His kissing did little to you, though!'

'How can you tell what I felt?'

His hands reached out to catch her shoulders and he pulled her towards him. She was too startled to resist as his ruthless mouth fastened on her lips, parting them helplessly. His hands slid down her back to her waist and held her prisoner, their grasp strong and yet not brutal. She had already felt the impact of his sexual power. Now that impact became irresistible, compelling her senses to awake in clamouring tumult. Lisa had never before experienced such an emotional onslaught. The calm procession of her days had left her untouched by passion in its most potent form. Now she came alive to realise what a world of powerful emotion lay beyond the halcyon waters of her former experience.

When Matt at last moved away she was dazed, her lids still closed, her mouth stinging with pleasure and a pain beyond pleasure.

'There,' he said huskily. 'Now tell me that fellow's kiss meant anything like that!'

She drew a parched breath and opened her eyes. The light seemed to hurt her sight. She saw his dark face dimly.

'Why did you do that?' she asked in a shaking whisper. Then, before he could answer, 'I'll tell you why, shall I? Your vanity is so monstrous that you couldn't bear to think that any man could be more attractive to a woman than you are ... every woman you meet has to be bowled over. You scatter your favours liberally because you have to see yourself as the irresistible, the unforgettable Matt Wolfe. ...'

'Thank you,' he said grimly as she paused for breath.

'I haven't finished yet!' she said furiously.

'I have!' he said, starting the car.

'I ought to slap your face, but I would hate to stoop to the same brand of cliché you seem to revel in ... stagey gestures mean nothing to me.'

'I'll take the slap as intended,' he said, apparently calmly intent on the road.

'Just remember ... never do that again! Or cliché or not, I'll give you a slap that will send you reeling!'

He gave a short, hard laugh, his face still enigmatically in profile, his eyes fixed on the road ahead.

Lisa was infuriated by the laughter. It made her threat sound so ludicrous, something uttered in childish rage, a gesture as melodramatic as his kiss. It made her feel silly, and hurt self-esteem brought a dark red colour to her face and made her brown eyes fierce with temper.

Sinking into her seat, she was silent for the rest of the drive back to her home. She was feeling very young and foolish for the first time in years, an emotion so startlingly new to her that she was confused by it into an acute dislike for the man who had caused it.

She had not felt really young since the day her mother died. That death had catapulted her into maturity. A rather young and sheltered seventeen, she had assumed management of a household overnight, shedding her adolescence like a snakeskin. There had been no time for a slow approach to adulthood. She had missed all the intermediate period, with its fun and its mistakes. Forced as she had been to assume a shell with which to deceive her father into believing her an adult, the shell had hardened around her over the years. Peter had accepted the shell, too, as deceived as everyone else.

Now, in a second, Matt Wolfe had stripped away the hard outer mask. She knew herself to be very inexperienced, very gauche, unable to cope with this dynamic man from a world she had never known. She felt like a trembling adolescent after a first kiss, and her uneasy confusion was painful to her.

They pulled up outside her home with a smooth sound. Fran's face peered from the window. Then she was running down the path, smiling delightedly.

'Well, hi!'

Matt Wolfe came round to open Lisa's door. As she slid out, wondering if her legs would still support her, she briefly met the dark blue eyes. They were icy cold, unsmiling. She shivered.

He turned away to greet Fran. 'Guess who's coming to lunch?' His tone was light and friendly.

'You? That's fantastic! Where did you meet Lisa? We were beginning to wonder if she'd got lost.' Fran looked at her with narrowed, suspicious eyes. 'We didn't know what to do about lunch, Lisa. I hope it isn't ruined.'

'I'll see to it,' said Lisa, moving away from them with Robby at her heels.

They followed her at their leisure, talking easily. She heard Fran laugh aloud. Her sister had no difficulty in meeting him on his own ground, Lisa thought grimly, walking through to the kitchen. She shut the kitchen door and began to work deftly, relieved to be back inside her shell, doing the things she knew best. She felt safe here. Familiar things surrounded her. She had tasks to do which she knew she was well equipped to perform. It was a question of security. For a moment Matt Wolfe had demolished her secure barriers. Now she hastily rebuilt them in the only way she knew.

When the meal was almost ready she went through to the dining-room to lay the table. As she moved around the room, her face intent, she could hear Fran's voice and the answering masculine laughter from their guest. She resented the easy familiarity between them. Fran is far too young for him, she told herself, placing the cutlery in position with great care. Yet wasn't Fran closer to him in experience than she was? Fran, left free to taste life, to flutter from one thing to another without the grim hand of responsibility holding her back, had more knowledge of the world already. Fran had a gay gloss of sophistication acquired during the last few years. Remembering the kiss she had witnessed, Lisa bit her lip. Fran hadn't been thrown by Matt Wolfe's kiss. She had taken it in her stride.

A tap on the dining-room window made her start. Peter's face grinned at her. She went over to open the window, smiling with pleasure. She was deeply glad to see him.

'I rang a couple of times, but they said you were still out walking. You must have gone a long way today. Did you feel the need to get out?'

'I walked up to Storm Dance and found Matt Wolfe up there,' Lisa explained. 'He's staying in the house planning the decorations. All he had was cheese for lunch, so I asked him to lunch with us.'

Peter's face lost its smile. 'I don't like that chap. Is he chasing Fran? You shouldn't let her go out with him. He's far too old for her.'

'Fran is twenty years old. How can I stop her? She wouldn't listen to anything I said anyway.'

'I've told you before, you've spoilt that girl. She's far too wilful and headstrong.'

Lisa smiled at him. 'Why don't you stay to lunch too? There's plenty for six. Fran picks at her food. I always have a lot left.'

Peter hesitated. 'I'd have to ring my mother.'

'Come round and do it now.'

He smiled. 'OK. What is for lunch?'

'Roast beef.'

'Marvellous! I love your Yorkshire pudding. Even my mother can't make it any better.'

'Goodness, you'll turn my head,' she said lightly.

Peter grinned and disappeared from the window. Turning back into the room, Lisa found Matt Wolfe leaning in the doorway.

For a moment the shock of seeing him made her freeze, her face unconsciously going white.

What's the matter with me? she asked herself desperately, trying to recover her composure. I'm making a fool of myself with this man. What must he think? It must be obvious that he has a shattering effect on me. He's far too experienced to miss it.

'Can I help you in any way?' he asked coolly.

She blinked, finding the question incomprehensible in her state of trembling confusion.

A faint smile touched the hard mouth. 'With the lunch,' he added blandly, the blue eyes humorous.

'No ... no, thank you....' She looked round the room. Everything was in place. Then she checked again. She must set another place for Peter. She moved back to the table and quickly did so, aware of Matt's eyes on her back.

'Do I gather you have another guest for lunch?' he asked softly to her averted head.

'Yes—Peter. He's just ringing his mother now.'

She walked towards the door, waiting for him to move out of her way. He made no attempt to budge, watching her in his lazy, graceful fashion, still with that ironic little smile.

She halted in front of him, flushed and uneasy. 'Excuse me, please. I have to serve lunch now.'

Slowly he moved out of her way just far enough for her to squeeze past. Lisa swallowed, glancing down, away from the bright blue challenge of his eyes, then walked past him and darted into the kitchen.

CHAPTER THREE

DOCTOR BAYNARD accepted the arrival of two guests for lunch with perfect composure. Peering over his spectacles at Matt Wolfe, he smiled vaguely. 'Haven't I seen you somewhere before? Are you one of my patients? I'm sorry I can't quite place your name, but there are so many ... and you look very healthy. I don't imagine I've seen much of you in my surgery.'

Fran giggled. 'You haven't seen anything of him, Dad. This is Matt Wolfe.'

'Oh, a friend of yours?' Doctor Baynard still hadn't connected the name or the face, but he was unperturbed. Fran had so many men friends. They had come and gone for years now. Some he remembered, some he didn't.

'Matt Wolfe, the TV star, Dad,' said Fran, embarrassed by her father's failure to place the name.

Matt Wolfe looked calmly at her. 'Why should your

father know my name? I expect he's far too busy to watch television.'

Doctor Baynard frowned thoughtfully. 'Matt Wolfe ... it rings a bell, certainly.'

'*The Squad*, Dad,' Fran prompted. 'That police series on Thursday nights.'

'Ah, Thursdays,' Doctor Baynard said regretfully. 'The night I listen to those third programme concerts. They're doing a series of my favourite symphonies this year. I never miss one if I can help it. I did miss the Mahler night. That was when Mr Kirk had his heart attack. I saw him in town yesterday. He's looking very much better. He's lost a lot of weight and his colour is improved.'

Lisa came in with the large soup tureen. She placed it on the sideboard and began to serve the soup. Fran grinned at Matt Wolfe.

'Dad lives in a little world of his own.'

'Don't we all?' His gaze was fixed on Lisa's calm face. She served Peter with soup, smiling down at him over his shoulder. Peter briefly touched her fingers as she moved away.

'So you appear on television,' Doctor Baynard murmured, breaking a roll into pieces. 'That must be an exciting job.'

'Not very,' said Matt. 'There's a lot of tedium involved in it. A lot of waiting between scenes, hanging about in the make-up department, watching while the floor managers fight over minor problems. I always make sure I've got a good book to read; a friend of mine listens to cricket in the summer. We all have our own way of passing the time.'

Lisa served his soup, carefully avoiding a look at him. 'Thank you,' he said drily to her averted face.

'Matt used to be a racing driver,' Fran said eagerly to her father. 'He has a fantastic car.'

Doctor Baynard looked up. 'Racing? Dangerous sport.'

'Highly dangerous,' Matt agreed. 'A young man's game.'

Doctor Baynard smiled. 'You consider yourself middle-aged, I suppose?' He was faintly teasing now.

'I consider myself too old to go on racing,' Matt admitted. He smiled back at the doctor. 'My reflexes aren't good enough.'

'You look very fit,' Doctor Baynard commented, considering him with a long glance.

'I hope I am,' Matt agreed. 'I need to be in my job. This series can be pretty exhausting. We do a lot of tearing around. Even though our fights are carefully staged, they take a lot out of us. We have to run through them a number of times to get them right, and that's very energy-consuming. Even waiting around uses up nervous energy. I sometimes think frustration is more demanding than the most furious action.' Again the bright blue eyes moved to Lisa's face, as if looking to see her reaction, but she was apparently intent on her own soup now, her bright chestnut head bent forward in reverie.

Peter had finished his soup. He sat back, staring at

Matt with dislike. 'I shouldn't think you knew much about frustration,' he said suddenly. The tone was so hostile that Lisa looked up in alarm.

Matt smiled lazily. 'It depends on the sphere, surely. I meant frustration in the sense of waiting to get on with my work. What did you mean?'

Peter's face flushed. 'I . . .' His words seemed to get stuck in his throat. He could not quite bring himself to say precisely what he had meant.

Fran laughed with a silvery tinkling sound. 'I guess Peter was getting at you . . .' she told Matt.

'I thought that myself,' Matt drawled.

Lisa hastily got up and began to collect the soup plates. Matt rose and helped her before it had occurred to anyone else to do so. Peter said crossly, 'Let me help, Lisa.'

'Too late,' Matt said mockingly. 'I've already volunteered.'

'Let Peter help,' Fran said hurriedly. 'He knows where things are. He's used to helping Lisa.'

Matt carried the soup plates out to the kitchen, ignoring her. Peter, half out of his chair, stared angrily at his retreating back. Doctor Baynard, blissfully unaware of the tension, gave Peter a smile.

'How is your mother?'

Trapped by the necessity to answer politely, Peter sank back into his seat. Fran drummed her fingers on the table, chewing on her lower lip. After a moment she got up and followed the others into the kitchen.

'I'll carry something in for you,' she told Lisa, who

was quickly taking plates out of the plate-warmer.

'You can take these,' said Lisa, handing them to her.

Fran mutinously had to accept them and return to the dining-room, feeling that she had been out-manoeuvred.

'Do sit down again,' Lisa told Matt. 'I can manage. I'm used to doing this.'

'Many hands make light work, my mother always tells me,' he said, his face amused.

She glanced at him in surprise. 'Your mother?'

'Even I have a mother,' he said mockingly.

She flushed. 'I didn't mean. . . .'

'Oh yes, you did,' he said. 'You see me with a tail and horns, don't you? Well, I do have a mother, and a father. By an incredible coincidence my father is connected with medicine, too.'

'A doctor?' She opened her brown eyes very wide.

'No, he works in the admin. department of St George's hospital, where he's a very minor cog in the medical machine,' Matt said drily. 'He still loves working there. He finds medicine fascinating. He wanted me to be a doctor, but I have absolutely no interest in the job.'

'That must have been very disappointing for him.'

'Yes, it was. He still broods over it occasionally.' He grinned at her. 'He regards my present career as purely temporary. He can't believe anyone would pay me to act. He suspects there's been a mistake somewhere and that one day it will be found out and I'll get the sack.'

'Do they still live down at Pelly Bridge?' Lisa asked,

placing the food carefully into the heating compartment of her trolley.

She straightened to find herself so close to him that their bodies touched before she hastily moved back, her lashes fluttering in alarm.

He smiled. 'Yes, they still live in the same house.'

'They look picturesque, but I imagine they weren't very comfortable to live in,' she said, pushing the trolley in front of her as she moved away towards the dining-room.

'Why not come and find out this afternoon?' he asked. 'I meant to drop in and see my parents. I think they'd like to meet you. I don't often bring friends down to see them.'

She halted, her golden-brown eyes wide in amazement. 'Me? You want me to come? But....' The invitation had taken her so much by surprise that her words came out in stammering fashion.

'I think they would like you,' he said offhandedly.

She wondered if he intended to take Fran, too, and then thought of Fran's expression when she realised that he had invited her sister along. 'Well, I would have loved to come,' she began hastily, intending to refuse.

'That's settled, then,' he said, taking the trolley in a firm hand and pushing it through the dining-room door.

Lisa was horrified. He had taken her opening words for assent! She stared after him, lips parted on a protest, but he was already in the room and it was too late.

She hurried after him and began serving the main course, her cheeks very pink. Fran, her lower lip pouting, glared at her across the table. Doctor Baynard was talking cheerfully to Peter, who was looking like Daniel in the lions' den, wary and apprehensive.

Gleefully spooning horseradish sauce onto his plate, Matt plunged into a hilarious anecdote about his TV series. '... So the car dropped forty feet into the river and we had to get a block and tackle to raise it. Rather than waste time, the director decided to film the whole damned thing and find a slot for it, so the writers were told to write the scene into the episode. That meant they had to change the ending and we all had a lot of new lines to learn, so all in all it was pretty disastrous.' He pushed his plate away with a contented sigh. 'That was superb.' He smiled at Doctor Baynard. 'Your daughter is a wonderful cook. You'd better be careful, Doctor. I might steal her away from you.'

Doctor Baynard laughed. 'Lisa's a home-loving creature. I have no fears on that score.'

Aware of those bright blue eyes on her, Lisa stood up and began to clear the table again. This time both Fran and Peter leapt to her aid. Matt Wolfe lounged at his ease, watching them with a faintly amused smile.

Before taking her walk that morning, Lisa had made a blackberry and apple pie. The blackberries had been gathered in the lanes at dawn with the dew still on them—the purple berries were more likely to be maggot-free at that hour. Served with thick yellow Devon cream the pie was delicious. Both Peter and

Fran had second helpings, and Doctor Baynard shook his head at them.

'You'll need to take a long walk after that excess,' he warned humorously.

'Or do the washing up,' Lisa prompted lightly.

Fran and Peter both jumped up, and Lisa looked from one to the other of them with an astonished smile. Usually she had to browbeat Fran to get her to help. This sudden desire to be helpful was unprecedented.

Fran looked appealingly at Matt. 'We'll do it,' she said, her eyes full of sweet invitation.

Peter was already moving towards the door. He touched Lisa's arm. 'We'll do it, shall we?'

'Cooks don't do the washing-up,' Matt drawled. 'Lisa has done enough for one day.'

Doctor Baynard raised his eyebrows, but smiled at Fran. 'Yes, Fran, your friend is right. Lisa has done all the work up to now. It's your turn. As Peter has so kindly volunteered, you can help him with the washing up.'

Fran stared at Matt, her eyes stormy. Then she flounced out into the kitchen without a word. Peter followed her reluctantly. Matt stood up, extending a hand to Lisa.

'We'll take that drive now, shall we?'

She hesitated. 'What about Fran?' She had taken it for granted that Fran would be coming too.

'I invited you, not Fran,' he drawled.

She flushed, bewildered and faintly alarmed. Searching for an excuse, she gestured to her yellow sweater and old tweed skirt. 'I'm not really dressed for visiting people.'

'You look fine to me,' he shrugged. 'My parents would only be uneasy with someone dressed in a Paris model. They never meet any of my showbiz friends.'

Doctor Baynard was leaning back, watching them curiously. He gave Lisa a smiling glance. 'Go on, child, have a nice afternoon. The family won't collapse if you aren't here.'

Matt took her elbow in a commanding hand. 'Thank you, Doctor,' he said, steering her firmly out of the door.

As the front door slammed behind them, Frank flew out of the kitchen and ran to the window in time to see them drive away. She turned back to her father, her small face set in angry lines.

'Where are they going? What does Lisa think she's doing, stealing my boy-friends?'

'Boy-friend? I thought you only met him the other day,' said Doctor Baynard gently. 'He isn't your property, you know, Fran. He asked Lisa to drive over to see his parents, I gathered. And why not?

Pelly Bridge was ten miles away from Saintpel. The road curved along the coast, rising and falling like a fairground roller coaster, with the sea on the right hand and the steep, misty downs on the left. The sky this afternoon was growing brighter, a clear blueness spreading from the east. Below them Lisa could see the cruel needle-sharp rocks along the beach, dark with seaweed at the moment, because the tide was coming slowly in, the white-topped waves creaming along the lower level of the beach. Some children were running along the sand, a small terrier at their heels, barking. Some men were fishing from a rowing boat out in the bay. Further out, a small yacht sailed in the distance, the wind flapping her sails energetically.

'As a boy my greatest ambition was to have my own boat,' Matt said

'Have you got one now?'

'No. I've never had time. But I will buy one as soon as I'm settled in at Storm Dance.'

'Horses and boats....' Lisa murmured softly. 'A pleasant life.'

'I have to work hard to get it,' Matt commented drily.

'You're lucky to have the chance,' Lisa said.

He laughed. 'Blunt but accurate.'

She flushed. 'I'm sorry....'

'Why should you be? You're absolutely right. Every day I thank God I'm in work. An actor's life can be pretty thankless. More than half of us are unemployed.'

Have you ever been out of work?'

Not so far. I moved from stunt driving to acting without a pause. I had luck on my side.'

She stole a glance at him, observing the toughness of his face; hard angles of jaw and cheek, straight firm mouth, long nose. It was a face built for endurance, the fleshless austerity only lightened by the blinding blue flash of his eyes.

Suddenly he turned his head and their eyes met. Lisa flushed, instantly self-conscious.

'I'm afraid Fran is going to be cross about this,' she said nervously.

He raised an eyebrow. 'Why should she?'

Suddenly angry with him, she snapped, 'You know perfectly well why!'

'Do I?'

'Don't be absurd. Of course you do.'

'I've met Fran twice. I told you, I'm not her property. We're casual acquaintances, that's all.'

'Does Fran see it like that, though?'

He shrugged. 'I really don't care.'

'Do you always disregard other people's feelings like that?' Her tone was contemptuous.

'Other people's feelings are their own business. I have enough trouble with my own.'

'Have you got any?'

He gave her a long look. 'Oh, yes,' he said softly. 'One day I'll tell you about them.'

For some reason his tone made her grow flustered and uneasy. She looked away, trembling slightly.

'I find it interesting that you should be so concerned about your sister's reaction to our drive,' he drawled. 'I would have expected you to be worried about what Peter thought.'

She smiled. 'Peter trusts me enough not to worry.'

The car suddenly put on speed with a full-throated roar, passing a hay cart at going on for seventy miles an hour. Lisa's heart leapt into her mouth as she looked down the steep sides of the cliff at the rocky beach. They were dangerously near the edge. She gripped her hands together in her lap to silence a cry of fear.

The car slowed again. Matt looked sideways at her, taking in the tense position of her hands, the pale quivering lips.

'Did that frighten you?'

'Yes,' she said flatly, her voice husky.

He drew into the side in a layby and parked. She looked at him in bewilderment. He turned towards her, his arm sliding down the back of the seat, surrounding her.

'You can't marry Peter Farrell,' he drawled. 'You don't love him and I very much doubt if he loves you.'

'I know you're an expert on affairs of the heart, but I prefer not to hear your views, thank you,' she said angrily.

'What's the matter? Scared? Afraid I may force you to face some truths you prefer to ignore?'

'Certainly not!'

'What do you think you're going to get out of marriage to Farrell? The status quo? A peaceful, undemanding domestic arrangement, like the one you've got now?'

'It really is none of your business,' she snapped.

'You've got Farrell exactly where you want him—under your thumb, is that it?'

'What an unpleasant remark!' She flushed angrily.

'You aren't very good at facing hard facts, are you, Lisa? You've run away from them for years. I imagine you wouldn't even recognise them now if they walked up and hit you in the face.'

'What are you talking about?'

'I'm talking about you, and the fact that you are not and never have been in love with Farrell.'

'How can you possibly make a statement like that?'

'The last time we discussed this, I kissed you, remember?'

She turned her head away, unable to meet his blue eyes. He waited for a moment, as if expecting an answer.

Then he said drily, 'You remember, surely, Lisa? Or would you like me to refresh your memory? I'd be delighted.'

'Don't touch me!' she whispered in a shaking voice.

'Now that is a very interesting reaction,' he murmured. 'You're even more scared now than you were when I overtook that hay cart on the cliff road. I wonder why?'

'I'm not scared. I just don't want you to kiss me,' she said hurriedly.

'Afraid you'd like it rather too much?' he taunted.

'I'd hate it!' She turned to face him, feeling like a wild animal at bay.

His face was closer than it had been. She felt a wild fluttering in her chest as she met the impact of the blue eyes.

'You could be beautiful, do you know that?' he asked softly, lifting one leisurely hand to touch her chestnut hair. 'Your skin is superb. Those eyes of yours are gorgeous.' The long fingers moved across her cheek with the instinctive sensitivity of a blind man. She was held, hypnotised, watching him helplessly as he moved closer and closer.

One finger touched the corner of her mouth with the lightness of a butterfly wing. 'Lisa,' he murmured under his breath. 'Lisa. . . .'

Her head was spinning dizzily. A reckless feeling of pleasure swamped the promptings of common sense. She knew he was just amusing himself because he had nothing else to do at the moment, but the clamouring of her own needs silenced her still small voice of caution.

Her lids closed, her head tilted back. Immediately Matt lowered his mouth and their lips fused in a mutual explosion of passion. Lisa flung her arms around his neck, touching the dark hair, her fingers learning the shape of his head and neck, pulling him down closer, stroking his cheek.

A darkness more complete than any winter night enshrouded them. The moments lengthened. Their mouths explored each other, parted and hungry. Matt's hands were awakening pulses everywhere they moved. Lisa lost all sense of time and consequence. Matt demanded, and she responded, her body leaping with new sensations.

Breathlessly Matt drew back, looking down at her cloudy eyes. 'That's how you should look,' he told her thickly. 'A woman in love looks like that—bemused, enchanted. . . .'

'I feel ... drunk. ...' she said faintly.

He laughed. 'It's far less pleasant being drunk, believe me. You and Farrell never touched those heights, did you?'

A lorry droned up behind them. The driver gave a long hoot and put his head out of the window to whistle insolently at them. 'Nice work if you can get it!' he shouted before driving on.

Matt laughed.

Lisa suddenly became aware of herself again. Her tumbled hair, her smudged lipstick, her flushed face—she loathed herself with utter contempt. She had let him make love to her again, despite all that she had said. How many other girls had he 'taken up to the heights'? How many other girls had forgotten common sense in the potent spell of his arms?

She sat up and began to tidy herself with shaking hands. Matt frowned.

'What's up now? Did that fellow embarrass you? Take no notice, it was only harmless fun. He probably envied me.'

'I think we'd better go back home now,' she said stiffly. 'I don't think it would be a good idea for me to meet your family today.'

'Don't retreat into that damned shell of yours, Lisa,' he said angrily.

'You've made your point,' she said bitterly. 'All right, I find you attractive. I imagine most women do. That's how you make your living, isn't it? Selling yourself? They ought to put you into bottles. They'd make a fortune selling your sex appeal to middle-aged men!'

'Don't be sarcastic. It doesn't suit you.' His eyes were narrowed in anger now.

'What does suit me, Mr Wolfe? What exactly do you want from me? To fall into your arms whenever you whistle?'

'Precisely,' he drawled, a fugitive gleam of mockery in the dark blue eyes.

'Well, sorry! I have no intention of playing your sort of game.'

'Pity,' he said. 'You play it rather well.'

Hot colour rushed into her face. 'That's a rotten thing to say!'

'Oh, come on,' he said. 'We both enjoyed that kiss. You may not be very experienced, but your instincts are good.'

'And my instincts tell me right now that I ought to go back home right away,' she retorted furiously.

'Too bad,' he said, starting the car once more. 'We set out to visit my parents, and we'll damned well get there.'

Lisa sat back in her seat, seeing the futility of protest, and silently avoided his occasional sideways glances. They covered the rest of the journey without a single word being said. When he pulled up outside one of the little cottages near Pelly Bridge, he turned to look at her, his blue eyes coolly unsmiling.

'You aren't going to be offhand with my parents, I hope,' he said cuttingly.

She gave him an indignant look. 'I have better

manners than to make a public scene,' she told him icily.

'I'm relieved to hear it. Come on, then.' He gave her a second look. 'Your lipstick is smudged, by the way.'

She hastily got out her lipstick case and applied fresh pink lipstick. Matt produced a comb and ran it through her hair, his fingers gentle and deft. Then he tipped up her chin with one finger and studied her coolly.

'Yes, that's how you ought to look.'

His parents were already at the front door to greet them. Lisa followed him, feeling absurdly shy and nervous. His mother smiled at her as Matt pulled her forward, his hand clamped around her wrist in a possessive gesture.

Mrs Wolfe was a short, thin woman with curly dark hair and her son's bright blue eyes. Her face was kind, intelligent and warm.

Her husband was a good foot taller than her. His broad shoulders and leonine head gave him a distinguished look. His hair was silvery, his eyes grey.

'So you are Lisa,' said Mrs Wolfe, leading her into the little house. 'We wondered what you would be like.'

Lisa was bewildered. They could not possibly have heard of her from their son. Who could they be mistaking her for?

Mrs Wolfe insisted on taking her into the kitchen to see a new plant she had bought while Mr Wolfe was talking to Matt. Lisa admired the plant's silvery leaves, helped her hostess to make a pot of tea, sliced fruit cake and laid a tray. Together they returned to find Matt and his father arguing over football.

'No more of that,' Mrs Wolfe told them firmly. 'Lisa and I aren't interested in you and your football! Sit down, Matt. Don't loom, there's a good boy. Lisa, give him his tea. He'll have a slice of my fruit cake too.'

Matt meekly accepted both tea and fruit cake, giving Lisa a brief twinkling glance as he did so. She sat down beside him on the sofa, as commanded by his mother. In this house there was no doubt who ran things. Mrs Wolfe, her voice kind yet decided, seemed to see everything even when she wasn't looking.

'Lisa likes this house,' Mrs Wolfe informed her husband.

He lifted interested grey eyes to Lisa's face. 'We love it ourselves. Of course, it's very inconvenient, but it has such character. Modern houses are very nice, no doubt, but they look like little matchboxes to me. This house is old and eccentric—a bit like me,' he added, grinning.

'Don't boast, Dad,' said Matt, smiling back.

'What sort of job do you do, Lisa?' Mr Wolfe asked politely, looking at her again.

'I don't exactly have a job,' she admitted shyly. 'I run the house for my father.'

Mr Wolfe raised an eyebrow in a fashion which reminded her strongly of Matt. 'Ah, domesticated, eh? Matt, you've found a rarity here. There aren't many of them left.'

'Your mother is dead, dear?' asked Mrs Wolfe.

'Yes, she died when I was seventeen.'

'And you took over? That was very nice of you. Have you any brothers and sisters?'

'One of each,' she admitted.

'And I suppose they help you when they're around?'

'Oh, yes,' she said, aware angrily of Matt's sardonic smile.

'It must be very hard for you; a girl of your age likes to get out and enjoy herself,' said Mrs Wolfe. 'Do you miss being free to have a good time?'

'No,' Lisa said flatly. 'I enjoy it all.'

'Oh, her life is just one mad whirl,' Matt drawled.

She gave him a furious glare, but he grinned back rakishly, his brows lifted in satiric comment.

'Would you like to see the rest of the house, Lisa?' Mrs Wolfe asked her.

Lisa accepted, glad to escape from Matt's gaze. She followed the other woman up the narrow, winding little stairs. The house was crooked in design, leaning like a ship in the wind, the floorboards creaking underfoot with every step. The ceilings were uneven, the walls bulged. But there was a warm, homely atmosphere which Lisa loved.

'This is Matt's old room,' said his mother, throwing open a door.

Lisa peered interestedly around at the narrow bed, covered with a patchwork quilt, the shelf of boy's books, the battered little desk by the window and the row upon row of rosettes and small silver cups which decorated every spare inch of wall.

'I keep all Matt's cups here. It seems the best place

for them. I was so relieved when he gave up racing—I
expected him to be killed every hour of every day
while he was doing it. I still can't believe he survived it
all. His best friend was killed, you know, in that last
crash. I don't think Matt's ever got over it. They were
very close. Dai was a nice boy, far too nice for that
gaudy redhead he married. She used to come down
here with Matt at one time, dripping diamonds and
sex appeal, patronising us left, right and centre. She
didn't even know we noticed, I think. She was too
stupid. I was glad she didn't marry Matt, but I felt
sorry for poor Dai.' Mrs Wolfe sighed. 'I think he and
Matt quarrelled over her just before Dai was killed.
That was one reason why it hit Matt so hard, that
accident. He felt as though he'd caused Dai's death.'

'Is that why he stopped racing?' Lisa asked shyly.

Mrs Wolfe nodded. 'I think so. He never said anything to us, but we both suspected that that was the
reason. Of course, Dai's death hardly affected her. She
went on making films and being photographed at night
clubs as if nothing had happened. Now Matt tells me
he's making a film with her.' She snorted. 'Huh! He
must be mad, getting involved with her all over again.
That's why I was so pleased when he said he'd bring
you over to see us.'

Lisa looked at her hesitantly. 'He told you he was
bringing me? But he only asked me this afternoon!'

Mrs Wolfe smiled at her warmly. 'He didn't actually say when he would bring you. He just mentioned
you casually and said one day he would drive you

over here. He thought we'd like you.' She laughed indulgently. 'Of course, he knew we were hoping he would meet a really nice girl. The sort of girls he meets in show business aren't the sort of girls any mother wants her son to bring home. He could see I was anxious about him seeing too much of Livia Marlowe, so to prove that I needn't worry, he told me about you. Otherwise, I've no doubt, he would have kept you a closely guarded secret for months. Matt was always secretive, even as a boy.'

Secretive and devious, thought Lisa, understanding so much more now. So that was why he had insisted on bringing her here today. He had used her as a shield to cloak his real interest from his mother. Indignation welled up inside her.

It wouldn't have mattered so much if he hadn't kissed her like that. That had been unforgivable. No doubt he had hoped she would be sufficiently starry-eyed after that kiss to give his mother the impression that they were madly in love. That would have kept his mother happy for months.

She followed Mrs Wolfe downstairs again, her expression blank and courteous. Not for worlds would she have let Matt's parents see the seething rage which was possessing her. She was in the grip of a savage desire to hit him. As she met his smiling blue eyes she had to dig her nails into her palms to stop herself swinging out a fist at that angular chin.

After saying friendly goodbyes, he drove her away from Pelly Bridge, his face all smiles. He whistled softly as he drove, his long hands steady on the wheel.

After a moment he glanced at her, lifting one eyebrow. 'You're very quiet. Did you enjoy it?'

'Your parents are very charming,' she said flatly. 'So is the house.'

He caught the hidden inflection of savagery and his glance sharpened. 'What's wrong now?'

'You used me,' she burst out.

'What?' A dark red flush came up into his face. 'What are you talking about?'

'I'm talking about the reason you took me to meet your parents, the reason you wanted them to think I was someone special to you,' she said bitterly.

He drove in silence for a moment, his brows a dark line above the blue eyes.

'And what was this reason?' he asked at last, his voice non-committal.

'Livia Marlowe,' she said huskily.

For a while he said nothing else, then he gave an abrupt bark of laughter. 'You and my mother certainly got on well, I see. How much did she tell you about Livia?'

'As much as she knows, I expect,' Lisa said.

'Which is very little,' he drawled. 'My mother puts two and two together and makes a hundred.'

'I'll cap that,' said Lisa. 'There's no smoke without fire.'

'I thought you didn't like clichés,' he drawled.

'There are some situations which demand them.'

'And what my mother told you made you angry?' he

asked softly. 'Were you jealous, Lisa?'

This came too near the truth for comfort. She forced an angry laugh. 'Jealous? Of you? You're joking, of course. I barely know you, and what I do know, I don't like. You flirt with any girl who happens to be handy. You use people. You're vain, arrogant and selfish. Why on earth should I be jealous?'

The car put on speed. Matt drove with an intent, shuttered expression, his long mouth compressed, his eyes on the road. Lisa shot a horrified glance at the speedometer, gulped and shut her eyes. Not for worlds would she let him see how much she hated driving at such speeds.

When the car finally slowed down it was within sight of her home. She opened her eyes to find the familiar outline of the house flashing towards her.

Matt drew up with a squeal of brakes and sat there, his hands on the wheel, not looking at her.

She said politely, 'Thank you for taking me to meet your parents. I enjoyed it. I suppose I ought to be grateful to you for teaching me a necessary lesson about flirts, too, but somehow I'm too annoyed to be grateful just yet.'

'That's enough,' he said between his teeth.

'I haven't had much experience of men like you,' she went on as if he hadn't spoken. 'You're a bit like whisky. You have a rapid effect, but it soon fades away unless you take another shot, they tell me. And then if you have too much, life becomes hellish. Dad gets a lot of alcoholics in the surgery, and I have to type out their cards. They all suffer from appalling depression. Life is grey and tasteless to them. I'd hate to feel like that.'

'I've got the point, Lisa,' he said tightly. 'Stop there.'

'I suppose you found racing as exciting as whisky,' she said reflectively. 'But even that palls in time, doesn't it? Glamour wears off. I prefer life without the tinsel. I'm not a tinsel type.'

He leaned across her and flung open the door. 'I'm not sitting here listening to this. Goodnight, Lisa.'

'I thought it was me who didn't like home truths,' she said sweetly. 'Don't you want to kiss me goodbye, Matt?'

'God, you're asking for trouble,' he spat suddenly, turning on her, his face black with rage. 'Do you want me to kiss you? O.K. But I thought you said you disliked me?'

'I detest you,' she said. 'I just want to prove something to myself.'

'What's that?'

'That I've been inoculated against you,' she told him calmly. 'I've had my injection. I'm proof against the worst you can do now.'

His eyes blazed. 'We'll see, shall we?'

He kissed her hard, his hands gripping her round the waist, but to Lisa's relief she felt none of the overpowering pleasure she had felt before. She kept her eyes open, looking over his shoulder at the darkening sky. The sun was setting behind the trees in an orange glow. Some starlings nesting in the trees flew up in a black flock and circled around against the brightness of the dying sun.

Matt drew away and looked at her unsmilingly.

Lisa gave him a hard, bright smile. 'Goodnight, Mr Wolfe,' she said, and got out of the car.

He slammed the door immediately and drove off so fast that she had not reached the gate before he had vanished.

CHAPTER FOUR

WHEN Lisa let herself into the house she was surprised to find Fran and Peter playing cards at the table in the sitting-room with apparent enjoyment. Normally they had no time for each other, snapping and snarling like hostile dogs when they met. She stood in the doorway surveying them incredulously.

Fran looked up and, amazingly, grinned at her. 'Where on earth have you been all this time? I was beginning to think Matt had abducted you.' She looked at Peter through her lashes, her pretty face mischievous. 'Peter was terribly jealous.'

Lisa had expected to be greeted with a furious denunciation when she returned. She had been looking for tears, for rage, for wild accusations—for anything but this light teasing.

'We drove to Pelly Bridge,' she explained, her tone

careful, 'Matt took me to meet his parents.'

Fran's eyes widened in disbelief. 'Why on earth should he want to take you there? How frightfully dull! What were they like?'

'Very nice,' said Lisa.

'I would have expected him to buy them a better house,' Fran said thoughtfully. 'He must be rolling in money. I wonder if he's mean? Rich people often are, they say.'

'What does Mr Wolfe's father do?' Doctor Baynard asked, laying his cards on the table face down.

'He works at St George's,' Lisa told him.

'A doctor?' Her father looked interested. 'What a coincidence!'

'No,' she explained, telling him about Mr Wolfe's job. He listened, nodding, watching her face with curious eyes which took in her high colour, her liveliness, with speculation.

Fran fidgeted irritably. 'Dad, are we going to finish this game or not? Hurry up! Lisa, make a cup of tea, will you, there's a dear. You're distracting Dad.'

Lisa strolled into the kitchen and heard them continue with the game noisily, arguing like children.

'I'm out,' Fran said triumphantly.

'Jam, pure jam,' Peter muttered. 'That's the fourth hand you've won in a row. I think you must be cheating.'

'Steady, children,' Doctor Baynard warned them, a smile in his voice.

'You're just a rotten loser,' Fran objected loudly.

'Not to mention a rotten card player.'

'I'll show you what a bad loser I am!' Peter said wrathfully. A moment later Fran's slender figure shot through into the kitchen, her eyes bright, her mouth curved in laughter.

'Help,' she gasped to Lisa. 'Hide me!'

Peter came into the room, his expression torn between amusement and determination. Fran sheltered behind Lisa, giggling. 'Save me from your mad boyfriend!' she cried as Peter dodged around to catch her.

'You wait until I catch you,' Peter snapped. 'I'll teach you to cheat at cards!'

The next moment he had dragged Fran out from behind Lisa, flinging her over his shoulder like a sack of coals, her legs kicking wildly. He carried her, shrieking breathlessly, from the kitchen out onto the long terrace which ran along the back of the house. Lisa, laughing, went on with making the tea. Through the window she saw Peter fling Fran into the old garden hammock which was slung there, setting it swinging violently.

Fran's voice drifted in through the window. 'You beast ... you horrible beast!'

Lisa covered the pot with the knitted cosy she had made herself, turning away to find the cups and saucers. She laid them out on the kitchen table, mentally counting the number who wanted tea, then went to call up to Timmy to ask if he wanted a drink.

'No, thanks,' he shouted back. 'What's all the racket going on down there?'

'Fran and Peter playing cards,' she called back.

'I thought it was World War Three,' he said calmly.

She went back into the kitchen to pour the tea and took it into the sitting-room. Her father had put a record on his stereo equipment. The gentle sadness of Dvorak's 'New World' symphony echoed around the room. Lisa kissed the top of her father's head as she placed his cup in front of him.

'There you are. Drink that.'

He lifted the cup to his mouth and sipped it pleasurably. 'So you enjoyed your visit to Mr Wolfe's home?'

'Very much,' she admitted. 'The house was charming. I can understand why they love it so much.'

He nodded. 'Money isn't everything, is it, darling? Life can be perfectly happy if you have just enough.'

She smiled at him 'You certainly are,' she agreed. 'Give you a comfortable home and a little music and you're in heaven, aren't you?'

She looked at the other cups, cooling on the table. 'Where on earth are Fran and Peter?' She went out into the kitchen to call them and Fran shot into the room, her face very flushed, her eyes bright with temper.

Lisa's heart sank. Had Fran quarrelled with Peter again? She hated to have the peace of the house disturbed by squabbles. 'Your tea ...' she reminded Fran.

'Don't want any,' Fran snapped, vanishing upstairs.

Timmy sauntered along the hall, chewing a toffee. 'What's up with Fran? She looks as if someone had tied a tin can to her tail.'

'I've no idea,' Lisa sighed.

'I'm going to bed early,' said Timmy, abandoning the discussion. 'I've got to get up at crack of dawn to deliver my papers.'

He had a newspaper round in the local streets, earning a considerable amount to supplement his weekly pocket money. Timmy was saving up to buy himself an expensive racing bicycle. Still at school, he spent very little money, preferring sports activities to girl-friends. Most of his spare time was filled up with homework. He was taking three A-level examinations which he was determined to pass so that he could go to university one day.

Lisa heard Fran's bedroom door slam shut and frowned. Why did Fran have to quarrel with Peter so much?

He came in from the terrace at that moment, his face as flushed as Fran's had been. There was a tight, angry look around his mouth which worried her.

'I'm going,' he said tersely.

She was astonished. 'So early?'

'I've some homework to correct,' he said abruptly, and walked towards the door.

Lisa followed him, expecting him to kiss her goodnight, but he avoided her eyes and left with a muttered farewell.

She watched him disappear with an anxious face. Was it possible that Peter was annoyed with her after all? Had he been jealous because she went out with Matt Wolfe? He had shown no signs of it at first, but then he was sometimes oblique in his reactions. He might have suppressed any feeling of jealousy, only to have it rise up again later when he had had time to think.

When he had gone, she joined her father in the kitchen. He was inspecting the remains of the roast beef with resignation.

'I might as well have some of this for supper,' he told her. 'Make a salad to go with it.'

'What about Fran?' asked Lisa anxiously.

'Where is she?' Doctor Baynard asked in return. 'I expect she wants something if she's going to stay in tonight. Has she got a date, Lisa?'

'I'll go up and ask her,' Lisa said reluctantly. She did not look forward to an argument with her sister.

When she tapped on Fran's door her sister answered in an oddly muffled voice, 'I'm changing.'

'Will you be in for supper?' Lisa asked through the door. 'I'm afraid there isn't much choice. You could have roast beef and salad with us, or if you like I could do you some scrambled egg on toast, or perhaps an omelette.'

'No, thank you,' Fran called, her voice clearer. 'I'm going out later.'

Lisa hesitated. 'With Tony?' She did not ask herself why her heart should miss a beat at the unbidden thought that Fran might have a date with Matt.

'No,' Fran said flatly.

Lisa ran her tongue over her dry lips. Why on earth did she feel so incredibly nervous suddenly?

'With Matt Wolfe?'

Fran's voice sounded wearily irritable. 'For heaven's sake, Lisa, stop cross-questioning me! What business is it of yours who I have a date with? I can go out with Jack the Ripper if I like, can't I?'

'I'm sorry,' Lisa said quietly. 'I didn't mean to probe.'

'Then just leave me alone,' Fran snapped. 'Anyway, if you can go off with Matt Wolfe without a word, why should I have to account for my whereabouts every minute of the day?'

Lisa sighed, admitting the justice of the accusation. 'I'm sorry if you resented my going with him,' she said gently. 'There was nothing to it. I think he did it on impulse.'

Fran opened the door. She was wearing a startlingly daring black dress Lisa had never seen before, the skirt very brief and tight-fitting, the bodice cut rather low.

Lisa's eyes widened. 'You're not going out with Matt Wolfe in that?'

'Why not?' snapped Fran dangerously.

'It's ... it's an invitation to rape!' Lisa gasped.

Fran tossed her head, her eyes scornful. 'You've got a very nasty mind, Lisa.'

'So has Matt Wolfe,' Lisa murmured drily.

Fran passed her and went out, slamming the front door behind her. Lisa joined her father in the kitchen and prepared their evening meal.

'Fran gone out?' Doctor Baynard asked casually.

Lisa nodded. 'Dad, is Fran cross with me because I went out with Matt Wolfe?'

'I've no idea,' he shrugged.

She sighed, staring down at the food she was preparing with a weary expression.

Her father watched her thoughtfully. 'You look tired to death. Why don't you have a holiday?'

She looked round at him, her expression incredulous. 'Dad, what on earth are you talking about? How on earth could I go on holiday? On my own, you mean? At this time of year?' She smiled. 'In case you hadn't noticed, Dad, it is autumn. And who would look after the house while I was away?'

'Don't let that bother you. We'll manage. Fran can do most of the cooking. It's time she tried her hand at managing a house. We've been very selfish. We've let you carry everything for far too long. You deserve a break.'

She was tempted, staring at his face intently. 'But where would I go?'

'I suggest London,' he said. 'You've lived beside the sea all your life. Time you took a look at the big city.'

'London,' she said faintly, her eyes dreamy. St Paul's, Westminster Abbey, the West End with its shops and restaurants, the Tower of London and Buckingham Palace. She had been there before, of course. She knew her way around the sprawling metropolis. She had never been there alone before, though, and suddenly the idea became exciting.

Doctor Baynard laughed. 'I see the idea appeals to you. Good!'

'When shall I go?' she asked.

'No time like the present,' he shrugged. 'Tomorrow morning I suggest you ring up a few hotels and book yourself into one of them for a week.'

'A week! That long?'

'If you enjoy yourself you can even stay on for a fortnight,' he said, grinning. 'Buy yourself some new clothes. Go to the theatre. A few concerts, maybe? Whatever you like. I'll write you a cheque to cover any emergencies.'

She hugged him. 'You're wonderful! It's just what I need at the moment!'

'Yes, I thought it might be,' he said smoothly.

She looked at him enquiringly, flushing. Did he suspect the turmoil which was churning around inside her? Had he some idea of the effect Matt Wolfe had had on her?

Doctor Baynard's eyes were calmly affectionate. 'I want you to be happy, Lisa.'

Next morning over breakfast she broke the news to Fran, who looked at her with wide, horrified eyes. 'Going away? Lisa! Why?'

Lisa was puzzled by her sister's tone. 'For a holiday in London to buy myself some new clothes and do a few theatres. You won't mind taking over while I'm away, will you?'

'Oh, of course not. No, I'll be glad.' Fran stared at her as if trying to read what lay behind Lisa's serene expression. 'But ... nothing is wrong, is it? You ... you haven't quarrelled with Peter? Last night....'

'Quarrelled with Peter? No.' Lisa flushed. Had Peter been furious with her for going off with Matt Wolfe? Guiltily she asked, 'Why? Did he seem annoyed with me?'

'Annoyed? No,' said Fran hurriedly. 'I just thought. ...' She broke off, her eyes widening. 'Oh, you mean because you went for a drive with Matt?'

'What else?' asked Lisa in bewilderment.

Fran flushed deeply. 'Well, he was a bit annoyed, but I think he got over it.' She moved her hands restlessly, pushing back her curls. 'I must rush. I have to get to work on time today. The editor has started making remarks about punctuality.'

'But it will be all right for me to go to London? You do think you can cope?' Lisa asked, following her out into the hall.

'Of course I can cope. Go ahead and book up,' said Fran. 'When are you leaving?'

'I haven't decided. It depends whether I can get a room somewhere or not.'

'You should be able to at this time of year!'

'Well, we'll see.'

'Shall you look up Cherry?' asked Fran on impulse, as she turned away.

'Cherry!' Lisa's face lit up. 'I'd forgotten ... she's in London now, isn't she?'

Fran nodded. 'She got back from Tokyo last month, don't you remember? She sent us a card the day she got back, giving us her new address. Where did I put that?' Fran frowned, chewing on her little finger. 'I know! In the letter-rack....' She rushed off to get it and returned, throwing it to Lisa. 'There! Give Cherry a ring this morning and fix up a lunch or something.'

'I'll do that,' said Lisa, looking at the card.

When Fran had gone, she picked up the London directory her father had produced from his surgery and flipped over the pages in search of a good hotel. The first three she tried were scornful. 'A room for a week? Oh, no, madam....' Feeling disconsolate, she decided to ring Cherry first. She needed cheering up.

Cherry was ecstatic at hearing her voice. She had been Lisa's best friend at school, but they had seen little of each other since Cherry took up a job with a Japanese shipping firm.

'Coming to London, darling? Super!' Cherry, since leaving school, had acquired an affected English accent with an aristocratic drawl she had never possessed as a girl. It helped, she told them, to sell her to her Japanese contacts, who expected her to talk like this.

'Where will you be staying?' Cherry demanded later.

'I haven't booked up with a hotel yet,' admitted Lisa. 'I'll ring you when I arrive and let you know.'

'But, Lisa darling, you can stay here! My flatmate is off to New York today for a month. You can have her room.'

'Oh! That's very nice of you, Cherry, but your friend might not like the idea.'

'Of course she will, silly one! Sometimes she's away for six months and then she sublets it to someone.'

'Perhaps I could pay her?' Lisa suggested nervously.

Cherry laughed. 'Don't even suggest it! While I was in Tokyo she found us a new flat and when I got back there was an airline hostess living in my room. Believe me, Jenny won't mind. You've got my address, haven't you?'

'Yes.'

'Then just pop along here when you arrive. I'll tell the porter to let you into the flat. He'll be in the cubby-hole downstairs in the entrance lobby. Make yourself at home if I'm not in ... darling Lisa, longing to see you. I must dash now, I'm late for work.'

When she had rung off, Lisa sat down to contemplate a whole week in London, her eyes like candles in her flushed face. She felt as if she had won the football pools ... sudden, glorious riches lay before her so unexpectedly!

After morning surgery she made her father some coffee and sat beside him, excitedly telling him about Cherry's suggestion. He smiled, watching her face.

'And you're going tomorrow?'

'So soon?' She had not considered an actual time of leaving, and her eyes widened in apprehension.

'The sooner the better, don't you think? Don't delay, Lisa, or you may never go. You know how routine can tangle one into knots. Cut through it with a sharp knife. Go tomorrow.'

'I suppose I could....'

'Of course you can.' He put down his cup and stood up. 'I must get on with my rounds. Pack your case, my

dear, and make a list of necessary instructions for Fran.
You need this holiday and you deserve it, too.'

She took the coffee cups through to the kitchen and
washed them up automatically, her mind abstracted. A
firm knock on the door startled her out of her trance.
She dried her hands and went to see who it was, half
expecting to find some anxious patient on the doorstep.

It was Matt, wearing a heavy black sweater with a
polo neck and black trousers.

She blinked at him, too surprised to say anything.

From behind his back he produced a bunch of dark
red roses, still just swelling out of their tight bud, their
scented hearts dew-sprinkled.

'A peace-offering,' he said gravely.

Lisa took them automatically, her eyes huge. 'Thank
you.'

He glanced past her into the house. 'Aren't you going to offer me a cup of coffee?'

She hesitated. She did not want to have him near
her. It hurt just to look at him, although she preferred
not to ask herself why. She despised him, she reminded
herself. He was contemptible, a flirt, an oversized ego
walking around in a far too attractive body.

'I can't apologise on your doorstep,' he said softly.

'No need to apologise,' she said, her eyes fixed on
the roses. The colour of blood, she thought, dark red,
dramatic.

Suddenly he lifted her by her elbows, like a stiff-
jointed doll, moving her out of the way so that he could
come in and close the door.

'Well, really!' Her face was suffused with hot colour. 'You have a nerve!'

'I was always told that when you met an immovable object you moved it,' he said mockingly. The handsome, sardonic face twinkled down at her. 'Now, about that coffee....'

Lisa knew when there was no point in fighting. Tomorrow she would be in London. She would not see him for at least a week. She knew she was secretly delighted to see him now, despite her dislike, her contempt.

'Oh, very well,' she shrugged, turning away.

He followed her down the hall to the kitchen, leaned on the wall and watched her making the coffee, her movements deft and accustomed.

'You do everything so gracefully,' he said suddenly. 'You make ordinary acts look beautiful.'

She flushed, surprised and gratified. 'Thank you!' No one had ever said such a thing to her before. Even Peter had always been critical of her appearance, slightly regretful that she was not better looking.

'You sound surprised,' he said. 'I don't know why you should. Surely even Farrell must have noticed how graceful you are?'

'He's never said so,' she said, shrugging a shoulder.

'The man's a fool. I suspected it, now I'm certain.'

'Don't criticise him!' She turned towards him now, her eyes angry. He had betrayed her yesterday into an act of disloyalty towards Peter. She would not make that mistake again. 'You of all people have no right to run him down. Peter is kind and decent.'

'And I'm not?' His mouth twisted.

'Well, are you?' Her eyes challenged him. 'What are you doing here, Matt Wolfe? Bringing me flowers, apologising ... isn't it all just to satisfy your own vanity? You hated me for telling you the truth. You want to make me take all those things back. You want to charm me into submission again.'

He moved towards her with a panther-like tread, his eyes holding hers. 'Do I? Could I, Lisa?'

'No,' she said, backing away. She turned and began pouring coffee with an unsteady hand. 'You're a dangerous sort of man, Matt. You love to be the centre of attraction. Any woman you meet has to find you irresistible and you'll go to any lengths to make her do so. I'm sorry for you. In a way you're pathetic. All that hunger for adoration. . . .'

'Adoration? Is that what you felt?' he asked mockingly, bending towards her.

She stiffened angrily and pushed his cup towards him. 'Drink that and go.'

He laughed. 'First I want to say what I came to say.'

'I don't want to hear it!'

'That's a pity, because you're going to have to listen.'

She turned away and walked towards the door, but he moved after her, caught her by the arm and swung her round to face him.

'Get your hands off me!'

'Just stand there and listen,' he said.

'I told you. . . .'

'Lisa, don't make me mad or I might lose my head and say or do things we'll both regret,' he said savagely.

'I regret I ever met you,' she retorted.

'All right,' he nodded, 'I know how you feel. You made that very plain yesterday. Now, will you listen?'

She drew a sharp breath. 'Well?'

'My mother has never liked Livia Marlowe. When she heard I was going to make a film with her, she was very upset. That worried me, because she suffers from angina and I didn't want to place any strain on her heart. So I thought that if I gave her the idea that I was seriously interested in another girl it might calm her down. I'd met you that first night—you looked the sort of girl my mother would approve of, so I told her about you.'

'Why couldn't you have made it Fran?' she demanded. 'Did it never occur to you that if anything got back to Peter, it might make trouble for me?'

'I couldn't tell her about Fran, to be honest, because my mother would no more approve of Fran than she does of Livia,' he said grimly.

'What's wrong with Fran?' Lisa was indignant now. She was fond of her little sister. How dare he imply that Fran was anything like Livia Marlowe!'

'Fran is far too young for me,' he said. 'What's more, she's shallow and very selfish. My mother's a shrewd judge of character. One look and she would have known all about Fran.'

Lisa flushed crossly. 'Fran's too good for you, in my

opinion, and you can tell your mother so!' She looked at him with loathing. 'And what about the consequences for me? It doesn't matter to you what harm you do to other people, I suppose? If Peter ever found out what happened yesterday he'd be furious!'

'Lisa, I meant what I said about him. Peter Farrell isn't fit to be your husband. He doesn't know you. He has no idea what you're really like.'

'You don't know what you're talking about! You've only met Peter a couple of times. How can you judge him on that?'

'I've seen him with you. He doesn't value you as you should be valued. You have qualities to which he's blind.'

She was silent, taken aback by the sincerity of his voice and eyes.

Quietly, he went on, 'Peter Farrell is one of those men who are taken in by the packaging. He wants a wife who's all tinsel and ribbons. Someone like Fran, in fact.'

She stared at him, her eyes opened to their fullest extent. 'Like Fran?' Suddenly a blinding light shone inside her head. She saw the past unrolling like a film. Peter looking at Fran ... Peter angry when Fran went out with other men ... Peter continually criticising Fran, jaggedly complaining about her, but always, watching her....

Taking her fixed stare for disagreement, Matt said thickly, 'You're too blind, Lisa. You won't see what's right in front of your eyes. Farrell has been going out with you for so long that the two of you never even talk any more. You've both altered over the years, but you haven't even noticed the changes in each other. What did he say when you got back yesterday? Was he jealous?'

She slowly shook her head. 'He ... didn't say a word.'

Matt spread his hands in an eloquent gesture. 'If my girl had gone off with another chap for hours I'd have had plenty to say, believe me! Lovers are jealous, Lisa. Lovers are blind, too—blind to the faults in those they love. Farrell isn't blind to your faults. He wants to change you, to make you ..iore like your sister.'

It was true, she realised. Peter was always saying just that, in one way or another. Why had she never realised it before? How could she have been so blind?

'And you,' Matt went on, 'do you really think you want a man who's prepared to wait patiently for years for you? If Farrell loved you, he'd sweep you off your feet, despite your protests, and marry you at once.'

Lisa wanted to be alone to think. He had broken up the pattern of her mind, the comfortable pattern on which she had intended to model her life, and she needed time to sort the fragments into some sort of new order. Confused thoughts were milling about inside her head. She felt disorientated.

'If you've finished your coffee I think you should go now,' she said coldly. 'I have a lot of things to do this morning.'

His mouth straightened in a grim line. 'You refuse

to listen, do you, Lisa? I thought you had enough brains and enough courage to see the truth once it was pointed out to you.'

'I don't want to discuss it any more,' she said, moving to the door and opening it.

His hand slammed it shut. Standing close beside her he looked down, his eyes blazing contemptuously. 'How much longer are you going to shut your eyes to the truth?'

'The truth? What would you know about truth? You kissed me yesterday and you hoped to cheat me into thinking you found me attractive ... why should I listen to anything you say?'

'Do you want me to admit I find you very attractive?' he asked huskily.

'I don't want you to do anything but get out of this house. I can forgive you for lying to your mother—your reason was understandable. But you had no excuse for making love to me. That wasn't necessary. If you'd told me the situation, asked me to help you convince your mother she needn't worry about you, I would have gone along with the pretence. You didn't need to lie to me.'

'I'm not lying,' he said. 'I wanted to kiss you.'

'Goodbye, Mr Wolfe,' she said flatly.

'Will you have dinner with me tonight?'

She gave him a look of astounded scorn. 'I will not!'

'Tomorrow, then?'

'Do I have to spell it out for you? I never want to set eyes on you again.'

'I don't give up easily,' he said. 'I'll be back.'

Lisa walked to the front door, opened it and stood there with a stubbornly defiant air as he walked through. He gave her a long, sardonic smile.

'I may have lost the battle, but I haven't lost the war,' he said softly.

She slammed the front door. Then she marched back into the kitchen, took his red roses and went out to the dustbin and rammed them into it, heads down. One or two of them broke and soft dewy petals floated away from them. Lisa felt intolerable grief at this destruction. She pulled them out again and looked at them, biting her lip. Poor things, they looked tattered now. She broke off one which was still perfect and took it upstairs to her bedroom. There she gently pressed it between the pages of a book of poems.

She packed her case, then sat down and wrote out a long list of instructions for Fran. Her father came back for lunch just as she had finished, and she had to prepare a scratch meal for the two of them.

The rest of the day flew past. In bed that night she wondered how she would feel when she reached London. She could not see herself away from Saintpel. Whenever she tried, the image dissolved. She had always been here, running her father's house, looking after her brother and sister, helping in the surgery. Her whole idea of herself was set in a rigid framework of habit. Now that framework was being pulled away and she had no idea what things would be like when it had gone.

She fell asleep at last, her mind still disturbed, and had strange unsettling dreams which lingered in her thoughts after she had got up and begun to make the breakfast.

Fran studied the list with a little frown.

'Do you think you understand it all?' Lisa asked anxiously.

'Of course I do. It seems quite straightforward,' said Fran. 'Look, stop fussing, Lisa. I can cope.'

Lisa was almost puzzled by Fran's helpful attitude. For so long Fran had been reluctant to help at home, skipping out of any work she was asked to do. Now she seemed eager to do everything, eager to get Lisa off to London, pressing her to go and forget all about the housework.

Doctor Baynard drove Lisa to the station before he set out on his rounds. The journey from Cornwall was a long one, and it would be late afternoon when she reached London. He urged her to make sure of a good meal on the train. 'Don't skip lunch, now. It will help to pass the time, don't forget. Have you got enough to read? Can I buy you some magazines?'

'I've got two books,' she said quickly. 'I don't need anything else. I shall enjoy just looking out of the window. It's so long since I went on a train.'

She kissed her father on the cheek and got into the carriage, arranging her books and her coat on the rack above. Her father slid her case in beside them, then got down onto the platform again.

'Enjoy yourself,' he said gently.

She leaned out of the window, waving until he was out of sight. Then she sat back in her seat and stared out at the fields as they flashed past.

She had not seen Peter to say goodbye. He had rung up in the evening to tell her he was busy with some work connected with an art exhibition, and she had told him about the holiday. Peter had seemed surprised, but he had not tried to talk her out of it. On the contrary, he had urged her to buy plenty of new clothes in London. Their conversation had been brief, almost formal. When he had rung off Lisa had turned to find Fran watching her anxiously, and the new suspicions planted in her mind by Matt had grown more likely as she met Fran's furtive glance.

'What did Peter say?' Fran had asked.

'Nothing much,' she had replied casually.

Fran had turned away, her face troubled.

Looking back, Lisa felt a new enlightenment. Was it possible that Fran was as interested in Peter as he was in Fran? Could the hidden attraction be mutual?

Were Peter and Fran aware of it, though? Or were they still hating each other on the surface?

She looked out of the window at the pale autumn sky, shot with filmy light, as delicate as a dragonfly's wing. Did all this exist, anyway? Or was it all merely the conjured myth of Matt Wolfe's devious mind? He had the actor's ability to convey a ring of truth even in his weakest tall stories. Somehow those cruel, beautiful blue eyes could compel faith. When he talked about Peter being attracted to Fran, somehow she had been forced to believe him.

A wave of cold shock ran over her. Had she even wanted to believe him?

Hadn't she felt a great relief at the thought?

All these years she and Peter had talked of getting married, had she ever really believed it, wanted it? Wasn't that why she had never made any real attempt to find a way out of her problems with her family? They had been an excuse all these years. She had used them as a shield against Peter.

The words were vaguely familiar as she thought them. Then she remembered, biting her lip.

Hadn't she accused Matt of using her, of making her a shield behind which he could hide?

She had been so bitterly indignant about it, yet she herself had been doing the same thing for years. People did use each other in that shamefully selfish way. She thought of herself hurling wild accusations at Matt and shuddered with distaste. How self-righteous could you get? No wonder he had been furious with her! It was really astounding that he had been generous enough to come round yesterday with flowers to make it up with her. And then she had compounded her offence by hurling the beautiful things into a dustbin!

Motives are so tangled and incomprehensible, she thought sadly. I'm not a very nice person, after all. All these years, turning myself into a martyr, pretending that I was sacrificing myself to the family, when I was just trying to escape from Peter. Why was it so hard to know oneself?

She opened her detective story, hoping to escape her own thoughts, but it was heavy going, forcing her way through the plot with her own life constantly bubbling up inside her head.

When they pulled into the London station she was still only half way through Chapter One, and none of the characters had become real to her.

She took a taxi to Cherry's flat. It was dusk, and the streets were crowded with people hurrying home from work early. The noise, the traffic, confused and alarmed her. The taxi swerved through the streams of cars, hooting sarcastically now and then. Pigeons flew up in grey spirals of beating wings. The glare of the yellow street lamps made the sky seem foggy. Shops began to glow with soft lights. She stared out of the taxi windows, trying to adjust to her new surroundings.

The taxi halted in front of a red-brick building. Lisa paid him, lifted her case out of the cab and stared up at rows of blank windows.

Pushing through the swing doors, she looked around the long lobby. A porter in a uniform advanced towards her, and she smiled at him nervously.

'I'm Miss Baynard. I'm visiting Miss Thaxted.'

He smiled politely. 'Of course, miss. She left a key for you at my desk.' He produced the key, gestured to the lifts. 'Her flat's on the third floor. Want me to come up with you?'

'No, that's all right,' she said with false confidence. 'I can manage.'

In the lift she looked dubiously at the panel, then pressed the button marked 3.

The doors slid shut and the lift rose with a soft

purring sound. When the doors opened again she found herself facing a long corridor. She walked down it, inspecting each door. At last she came to the one with Cherry's number on it.

The flat was surprisingly spacious—one long sitting-room with an L-shaped kitchen alcove; two small bedrooms and a bathroom. Putting down her case, Lisa crossed to the windows and found herself looking down into a darkening London street. A bare plane tree stood opposite. A street lamp gave a circle of yellow light.

Lisa drew the curtains and stood looking around the room. Well, she told herself, I'm here. This is London. She felt defenceless, a snail without a shell. For the first time in her life she was on her own, with no one to look after but herself, and no one who cared what happened to her. It was a devastatingly lonely experience.

CHAPTER FIVE

CHERRY was small and dark and vivacious, a girl who had cut her way through the world with her own talents and still cherished further ambitions. At school Lisa had never suspected that Cherry would do the things she had done. Cherry had been so popular, a honeypot surrounded by bees. Any boy in the school would have been delighted to date her. If Lisa had thought about it, she would have prophesied that Cherry would get married early and settle down as a happy wife and mother. Far from doing this, Cherry had gone to London, joined a large international shipping company with a home base in Japan, and spent the years since leaving school travelling around the world as a high-powered executive.

Kissing her warmly, Cherry gave a scream of dismay. 'Darling, your clothes! You can't go out like that! People would stare at you in the streets!'

Lisa glanced down at her skirt and sweater. 'Is it that bad?' she asked ruefully.

'Worse,' Cherry shuddered. 'I was being kind.'

Lisa laughed. 'Thank you!'

'Seriously, darling, you must get some new clothes. I was taking you to a party tonight, but I can't take you looking like a refugee from Oxfam.' She chewed her little finger thoughtfully. 'I know! You can borrow some of my flatmate's clothes. She's more or less your size—none of my clothes would fit you. You must be three inches taller than me!'

'Oh, I couldn't. . . .' Lisa began, but Cherry was already rummaging through the tall wardrobe which was fitted into an alcove of the room. She whirled round, holding out a long black dress.

'This should fit.'

Lisa took it doubtfully, holding it out at arm's length. It was made of some clinging material, silky and fragile. Something glittered along the hem, a faint trail of silvery dust sprinkled to make a pattern.

'Try it on,' Cherry protested. 'You can't tell by looking at it on a hanger!'

Lisa laid the dress down on the bed. 'Look, I'll skip the party tonight, if you don't mind....'

'Oh, but I do, darling,' Cherry said firmly. She took hold of Lisa's sweater neck. 'Come on, off, off, ye lendings!'

In a moment Lisa was stripped to her plain white slip. Cherry regarded this with distaste.

'What a dreary object! Where have you been living, Lisa? The North Pole? Well, never mind. I'll find you something better later. First things first.' She slipped the black dress over Lisa's head, twitched and adjusted it for endless minutes, then stood back and stared at her with a blank face.

Lisa looked back, anxiously. There was rather less of the dress than she had expected, rather less than she had ever worn before. There was no back, no sleeves and very little front. She felt naked, exposed, idiotic.

'I can't wear this! It's ... indecent!'

'That settles it, then,' Cherry sighed. 'It's perfect.'

'Cherry!'

'Darling, your taste is so awful that anything you find that terrifying must be good.'

'Let me see what it looks like,' Lisa demanded.

Cherry grabbed her arm. 'Not yet. First a bath.'

'A bath? I had one this morning!'

'Not this sort of bath you didn't,' said Cherry, removing the black dress from her with a whisk of silk. She pushed Lisa across the flat, turned on the bath taps and poured all sorts of scented, bubbly things into the water so that it foamed up like Niagara and the air was filled with a heady fragrance. 'Now,' said Cherry, 'soak for fifteen minutes. That will give me time to do a few jobs of my own.' She looked at Lisa's face closely. 'Thank God your skin is so good! You don't deserve it. I'll style your hair while I do your face.'

She slammed out of the bathroom and Lisa got into the bath. It was a delicious sensation, one she had never had before. Baths were functional in her experience. She had never known water so silky, so perfumed. After a while her skin seemed to take on the properties of the bathwater too, growing smoother and more scented with each moment. She lay back, sighing, closing her eyes.

Her hedonistic moments flew past. Then Cherry was in the room again, her face oddly white and stiff. 'Face pack,' she mumbled through tight lips. 'Get out.'

Lisa climbed out and was enveloped in a white terry towelling gown.

Cherry pushed her down onto a wicker bathroom stool and began to do things to her face with cotton wool and creams and lotions. Lastly she shampooed Lisa's hair with a shampoo which smelt of roses and apples.

'Sit still,' she commanded, producing a pair of scissors.

'What are you going to do?' Lisa was horrified. She put a protective hand up to her hair. 'No, Cherry!'

Cherry grimly pushed her hand down and began to

cut. Lisa gave up the ghost at that moment, watching her thick lustrous curls of hair fall down towards the floor.

Cherry made a little groan. She moved away towards the bathroom basin and began to wash her face pack off, with little splashing movements and soft dabs.

'I'll probably look like the ghost of Whistler's mother all evening,' she moaned as she dried her face with cotton wool.

Lisa had stood up and was staring at herself in the steamy bathroom mirror. Shorn and naked-looking, her face seemed thinner and pallid.

'What have you done?' she asked Cherry miserably.

'Wait and see,' Cherry retorted. 'Come on, we can clear up the mess later. The party starts at eight and we have lots to do before we leave.'

Lisa followed her like a lamb. Cherry found a hair-dryer and began to brush and dry Lisa's hair, whistling under her breath in a cheerful fashion which incensed Lisa.

The next few minutes passed like some incredible dream. Lisa was conscious of incredulity, of despair, of a wild belief that she was going mad.

At last Cherry pushed her towards a mirror. 'There!' she said, triumphantly.

Lisa looked. And looked again, searching for the familiar image, the reflection she usually saw.

It was absent. Instead there was this strange girl, slender, sophisticated, in a stunning black dress which clung wherever it touched and revealed vast amounts of white skin. Rich chestnut curls rioted all over the girl's head. Her white neck rose like a swan's from the barbaric glitter of a brass necklace, row upon row of metal cresent shapes which clinked and shone as she turned her head.

Lisa stopped breathing for a second. 'Is it me?' she asked faintly.

'Congratulations will be received,' Cherry crowed.

Lisa looked round at her, her golden-brown eyes huge. 'It's ... fantastic!'

Cherry grinned. 'Right. Now sit very still and don't even breathe. I have to work a similar miracle on myself.' She vanished into her own bedroom. Lisa sank into a chair and stared at her long, pale fingers, tipped now with scarlet, a colour she had never worn before, but which now gleamed on her lips and nails.

The door bell rang. Cherry, from her bedroom, shouted, 'You can answer it if you don't touch anything.'

Rustling to the door, Lisa opened it. Outside in the hall stood a tall, distinguished man with dark, silver-winged hair and cold grey eyes. He stared at her, then smiled.

'Well, hello! Is Cherry ready?'

Lisa hesitated. 'Not yet,' she said dubiously.

'Nothing new in that,' he said lightly. 'May I come in?' Then, seeing her doubtful glance, 'It's all right, she's expecting me. Will you tell her Adam is here?'

Cherry's voice yelled at that moment, 'If it's Adam give him a drink. He knows where it is.'

Lisa stood back and Adam passed her. He was wearing an extremely elegant dark suit and carried a cellophane-topped box under one arm.

'I'll pour the drinks, shall I?' he suggested, moving to a long Scandinavian-style cabinet. 'What would you like?'

Her mind was a blank. She just gazed at him dumbly. The grey eyes flickered with amusement.

'Gin and orange, I suggest,' he said softly. He poured a great deal of orange into a glass, added a little gin, then poured himself a rather larger amount of whisky into another tumbler and added soda. Turning, he handed Lisa the gin.

She took it doubtfully, wondering about this man and Cherry. He was much older than Cherry. She suspected him to be on the wrong side of forty, and so attractive a man could hardly have reached that age without getting married.

'Are you staying here long?' he asked.

'A week,' she answered shyly.

'You're Lisa,' he said.

'Yes.' She was astonished that he knew her name.

'Cherry told me about you.' He smiled at her, tilting his drink so that ice clinked against the glass. 'You're a doctor's daughter from Cornwall. I've always been absolutely unable to see Cherry against a Cornish background, but perhaps I was wrong. . . .' The grey eyes ran over her. 'What was Cherry like as a little girl?'

'Very pretty and very popular,' said Lisa.

'Especially with the opposite sex, I suspect,' he said drily.

Lisa laughed. 'Yes.'

'She hasn't changed,' Adam murmured. His grey eyes moved to the door of Cherry's bedroom. 'She hasn't mentioned me to you, has she?'

'No.'

'I guessed as much. Now I wonder whether that means that she's just indifferent to me, or whether it means she doesn't want to talk about me.'

'Cherry never talks about her men friends,' Lisa told him.

He sighed. 'She's a very annoying girl. I don't know where the hell I am with her. I feel like I used to when I was a boy, trying to catch a butterfly in my net. Somehow the creature always used to escape at the last moment.'

Lisa gazed at him curiously. Was he serious about Cherry? It sounded as if he was.

'Do you work in London?' she asked him politely.

He gave her a long, cool look. 'Changing the subject? Yes, I do work in London. I'm a barrister.'

'Goodness!' Lisa was impressed. 'How did you meet Cherry?'

'I specialise in mercantile cases,' he explained. 'I met Cherry when I took a case for her company.'

'You must have a fascinating life,' she said, very admiring.

'No, it's rather tedious,' he retorted. 'Cherry was the first attractive thing I'd run into for months.'

The bedroom door opened and Cherry joined them. She was wearing a short dreamy red dress which flared at the hips but fitted tightly over the bodice. She looked intense, dramatic, eye-riveting.

'Do you mind if Lisa comes along?' she asked Adam casually as he rose.

'Oh, it doesn't matter,' Lisa began to protest, horrified to realise that she was being added to Adam's party.

Adam turned to smile at her. 'I'll be delighted to have you with us,' he said in his cool, authoritative voice. 'I took it for granted that you were. This is a free and easy party. There'll be hordes of people there.'

'Come on,' Cherry urged, flinging a black lace shawl around her shoulders.

'Is that all you're going to wear?' Adam asked calmly.

'Your car is always so warm,' Cherry protested.

'What about Lisa?' he asked, glancing at the expanse of white skin revealed by Lisa's dress.

Cherry darted back into her room, came back with a short white angora jacket. Lisa slid into it and smiled at her.

'You're being very kind to me.'

Cherry grinned at her. 'It's a pleasure, kiddo.'

The party was being given in a tall, Edwardian house in Kensington. The whole of the ground floor was brilliantly lit. The sound of the music drifted out to them as they rang the doorbell. Someone opened the door, lifted a casual hand and vanished. They struggled inside, finding themselves crushed by a great throng of people.

'Who on earth is giving the party?' Cherry asked Adam.

He shrugged. 'Jackie Selkirk invited me. I suppose she is ... this is her house.'

Cherry giggled. 'Oh, well, tread boldly, men! Lisa, don't get lost ... hang on to my hand!'

They forged ahead through the other guests until they were in a long, high-ceilinged room decorated in palest apple green with gilded medallions on the ceiling and long, floor-length brocade curtains of gold material.

A few people hailed Adam. He introduced Cherry and Lisa to them. Lisa smiled and shook hands, failed to catch the names. There was room to move in this room, people were dancing to the music, their bodies so close you could not get a piece of paper between them. Cherry was suddenly greeted by a thin, shock-headed young man with a cheerful expression. While she was talking to him, Adam gestured to the dancers.

'Care to dance, Lisa?'

She glanced at Cherry, who gave her a wink. 'Go ahead, sweetie.'

Adam slid his arm around Lisa, pulled her close and moved in among the crowd. Lisa found that she could only move by leaning against him, her head on his shoulder.

'This is wilder than I expected,' he said into her ear. 'O.K. with you if we split?'

She turned, bemused, and found her nose brushing his chin. 'I'm sorry? I don't understand.'

He laughed. 'I picked the slang up from Cherry. I meant that the party is a little too crowded. Would you mind if we went on somewhere else?'

'Not at all,' she said, rather relieved. She was finding the experience trying. So many people in such a small space, all talking and shouting. . . .

Adam danced close to where Cherry was standing, hemmed in by the crowd. Leaning over, he shouted, 'Let's split!'

Cherry nodded at him. 'See you outside.'

Adam gave a quick, cold glance at the young man who was engrossing Cherry's attention, but didn't argue. He moved towards the hall again, carrying Lisa with him helplessly.

They pushed their way back to the door. Another moment and they were disgorged onto the pavement, blinking in the darkness, breathing in the cool night air.

'Thank God for that,' Adam said on a sigh. 'Bedlam, wasn't it?'

Lisa leaned on the gatepost, breathing deeply. She felt as if she had been deprived of oxygen for hours. Adam moved closer, looking down at her.

'Are you all right?' he asked anxiously.

'I am now,' she said. 'Surely they can't be enjoying themselves in there?'

'Incredible, isn't it? Like the rush hour in the underground.'

He looked back at the house, his mouth tightening in visible irritation. 'Where on earth is Cherry?' He looked at his watch. 'I'll wait for five minutes, then if it's all right with you, we'll go on to dinner.'

Lisa was horrified. 'Oh, no, we couldn't ... Cherry wouldn't know what had happened to us. I'm sure she'll come out in a minute. I expect she's talking to somebody.'

'Some man, you mean,' said Adam.

'Look, I'll go back and look for her,' Lisa offered, taking a deep breath in preparation for a dive back into the scrum.

Adam looked at her with a faint smile. 'No, you won't. You should see your face! Greater love hath no man than this, that a man should lay down his life for his friends ... would you really go back into that hell-hole for Cherry? She's right about you—you're one of the original English martyrs.'

Lisa winced, deeply wounded, remembering things that hurt.

Adam frowned. 'I'm sorry, did I hit a nail on the head? It was just a joke.'

Two more cars pulled up, and people climbed out of them, rushing up the steps like the Gadarene swine, talking, laughing, jostling each other.

Adam scooped Lisa out of the way with an iron arm, holding her protectively against him as they rushed past. She looked up at him pleadingly. 'Do wait for Cherry.'

'No,' he said flatly. 'I decided tonight that I was

tired of dancing attendance like a puppet. From now on if Cherry wants me she's going to have to come to me.'

'But she'll think that I....' Lisa broke off the sentence, stiff with embarrassment.

'That you?' He bent to look into her face, and a smile of impish amusement lit his stern face. 'That you lured me away, you siren? Well, why not? Let's see what a little jealousy will do.'

Lisa was aghast. 'I can't ... I couldn't ... not to Cherry!' Not another man preparing to use her to protect himself! she thought with rebellious dismay. Did people always use each other in this egotistic fashion?

A red sports car shot up the road and parked with skill. Adam edged Lisa towards his own car, his arm around her waist. 'At least wait in the car,' he said. 'It's freezing standing here.'

The door of the sports car opened as they passed. A pair of long legs appeared, then the driver straightened up, facing Lisa.

She felt a sudden jabbing pain under her heart. It wasn't possible, she told herself. She must be seeing things. Did the heart conjure up mirages to comfort itself?

Narrowed blue eyes stared, incredulous. Adam steered her past him, opened the passenger seat of his car just as Matt took three long steps towards them.

'Lisa?' His voice was savage. 'My God, what's happened to you? What have you done to yourself?'

She turned to face him, trembling. Adam's arm tightened, as though he felt the physical shock she had suffered.

'Hello, Matt,' she said, trying to sound at ease.

'A friend of yours, darling?' Adam asked softly. 'Aren't you going to introduce us?'

She barely noticed the 'darling' so mischievously thrown into the remark, but Matt noticed and gave Adam a look of undisguised hostility.

'Haven't I seen you somewhere before? Are you an actor?'

Adam raised his brows icily. 'I am not, thank God. I'm Adam Browning.'

'The Q.C.?' Matt's dark brows shot together in a ferocious frown. 'I didn't realise Lisa moved in such exalted circles.' He swivelled another icy look over Lisa, sweeping her from head to toe with eyes that expressed disgust. 'Are you responsible for this transformation?'

'Lovely, isn't she?' Adam returned sweetly.

Lisa wanted to get away. She needed to be alone, to burst into scalding tears. Somewhere at the back of her mind all the time had been a secret desire that Matt should see her in her new sophistication and realise that she was not just a country mouse. Her legs were going to give way beneath her if she didn't get away soon. She was shaking so hard she had to clench her teeth to stop it from becoming only too obvious to Matt.

'Sorry we can't stop,' Adam said suddenly. 'We're off to dinner now.' He thrust Lisa into the seat, slammed the door and walked round to get into the driver's seat.

Matt bent to stare at her through the window, tapping violently on the glass, his mouth moving. 'Lisa!'

Adam started the car, swung the wheel deftly. The car edged away from the curb. Lisa did not look round at Matt. Her hands were clenched tightly in her lap. Her eyes were burning with unshed tears.

The tears began to spill past her lashes, down her cheek into the corner of her mouth, leaving a salty taste upon her inner lip. She sniffled, brushing a hand across her eyes.

'Don't look now,' Adam drawled, 'but we're being followed.'

She sat up. 'What?'

'Don't look round,' Adam said, grinning. 'We'll ignore him.'

'Matt?' Why was he following them? She had thought him safely occupied in Saintpel, planning the new décor for Storm Dance. Why had he come to London so suddenly? She asked herself the questions knowing that she wanted to believe he had followed her to town, but not daring to believe it because it was so incredible and fantastic an idea. Matt had only been using her. He had no interest in her. Or had his vanity been hurt when she ran away like that? Was vanity his reason for coming after her?

'Quarrelled with him, did you?' Adam smiled sideways at her. 'Was he cruel to you?' He looks capable of cruelty.'

'Oh, he is,' she breathed, shivering.

'Then we'll teach him a lesson. Cherry has been cruel to me, so I know what it feels like.'

Lisa longed to look round to see if it really was Matt following them, but she dared not.

'You're in love with him, of course?' Adam asked.

'I'm not....' she gasped. Then, more honestly, 'I don't know...yes...no!'

'If I ever got you into the witness box I'd make mincemeat out of you,' Adam said reflectively. 'Your mind is in total chaos.'

She gave a slightly hysterical choke of laughter. 'I'd hate to face you across a courtroom! You talk about Matt being cruel, but I suspect you could be worse.'

Adam smiled, obviously flattered. 'Possibly,' he admitted. He spun round a corner with a screech of tires and pulled up beside a small French restaurant. Gay coloured blinds shaded the windows. A white tub held a bay tree.

Adam helped her out of the car, locked it, and shepherded her across the pavement into the restaurant. As they moved into the room and were welcomed by a bowing waiter, Lisa, with a sidelong glance out of the window, saw Matt's red sports car shoot down the street, pass Adam's car and brake. Then the red sports car backed slowly into place behind Adam's car and Matt leapt out, slamming the door.

Adam drew back a chair, and Lisa automatically sat down opposite him at a table for two. A purple candle shaped like a tulip burnt between them, casting a pale light across Adam's face. The room was faintly lit with reproduction antique lamps which hung from the wall but gave only the dimmest light.

The head waiter handed them each a menu, bowing obsequiously. Soft music oozed from a hidden speaker somewhere.

'Would you like an aperitif?' Adam asked her, leaning across to touch her hand with cool fingers.

She blinked at him, aware that at that moment Matt was opening the door behind them and standing, glaring across the room at them.

Adam's smile was amused. 'Yes, of course you would.' He ordered something. The head waiter moved away, leaving them to study the menu. Lisa gave Adam an appealing look.

'I can't stay here. Not with Matt watching me ... I couldn't eat a mouthful. I'd feel like something under a microscope.'

'Nonsense,' he said firmly. 'Where's your spirit? Ignore him. Concentrate on me.'

'I can't!' she wailed beneath her breath.

Adam took both her hands firmly between his fingers and stared at her intently. 'Now, listen to me. Cherry has already spoilt the evening, don't you follow suit. Your young Lothario can kick his heels all night if he likes, but I intend to enjoy my dinner, and I insist that you do the same.'

She knew he was right. She had to pull herself together. Seeing Matt so unexpectedly had thrown her. She lifted her chin. 'I'm fine now,' she said.

Adam's stern face lit with a smile. 'That's better,' he

said in satisfaction. He lifted her hands to his lips and kissed first one and then the other lightly on the back.

The waiter materialised with their drinks. Lisa sipped hers without even noticing what it was and felt a warm glow spreading through her. Adam was glancing calmly through the menu.

'Do you like sardines?' he asked her. 'We could start with sardine and tomato garni. . . .'

'Mmm, I'd like that,' she said dreamily, finishing her drink.

'What about coq au vin to follow?' he asked.

She nodded. 'Fine by me.'

Adam glanced at the waiter and nodded. A wine list was produced and Adam skimmed through that.

'As it's a special occasion I think we'll have champagne,' he said to Lisa.

She opened her eyes wide. 'Champagne? Goodness!'

He laughed and turned to the wine waiter, telling him which bottle he wanted. The waiter vanished and he turned back to Lisa.

'Alone at last,' he said softly.

She giggled, brushing back a stray chestnut curl from her cheek with a little gesture.

Adam followed the movement with lazy grey eyes. 'I wonder what you looked like before Cherry wrought her marvels,' he said slowly. 'Whatever it was, I gather your Lothario didn't like the change.'

She shrugged. 'He isn't my Lothario. I barely know him.'

Adam raised one brow. 'Tell me about him.'

'There's little to tell.'

'I recognised him, of course,' Adam said. 'That face is quite unmistakable. How did you come to meet him?'

She told him about Matt buying Storm Dance, and Adam put quick, shrewd questions to her, extracting more and more information, until he had heard the whole story. Without realising it, her expression told him as much as her words; her large golden-brown eyes glowing, her mouth quivering passionately, her lashes sweeping down to cover the emotions which came and went.

The first course came and they ate it as they talked. The wine waiter brought the champagne in its silver ice bucket, clinking with ice. He opened it, sending the cork shooting up into the air. With a bow he offered the cork to Lisa, who smiled delightedly, accepting it.

Then the coq au vin arrived. Lisa tasted the delicate pieces of chicken delightedly. Tiny slivers of mushroom, quartered tomatoes, diced carrot made the rich brown vinous sauce doubly delicious. From time to time the waiter topped up her glass, and she drank the champagne without realising how potent it was, enjoying the bubbles and the light, crisp bouquet.

'Go easy on that,' Adam murmured wryly. 'Champagne can go to your head, you know.'

She smiled mistily at him, over her bubbling glass. 'It isn't having any effect on me.' Except, she thought clearly, that I feel like singing and a funny shivering sensation of excitement is coursing through my veins. But that doesn't matter. Anything is better than the misery I felt earlier when Matt looked at me with such scorn and distaste.

The sweet trolley was wheeled up. She leaned over to inspect it and chose a piece of Brie in the end. Adam had the same. The coq au vin had been too rich to have anything sweet afterwards. The smooth, creamy cheese was perfect.

'I hope your friend isn't going to suffer from indigestion all night,' Adam drawled.

'Why?' Lisa asked carelessly, sipping black coffee.

'He hasn't taken his eyes off you since he sat down and he looks as if every mouthful revolts him.'

'Poor Matt!' she giggled. Somehow the picture amused her.

Adam surveyed her thoughtfully and clicked his fingers. The waiter filled her coffee cup again. When he had moved away, Adam said softly, 'You need as much strong black coffee as you can drink.'

'I'm not drunk!' She looked at him with muzzy indignation. 'I'm not a bit drunk!'

'No?' Adam gave her a dry little smile. 'All the same, I think I'd better get you back to Cherry's flat now. Have you got a key?'

She fumbled in her handbag, dropping it to the floor, sending objects rolling away crazily. Adam came round to help her pick them all up. Kneeling on the carpet, supporting herself by leaning on Adam's arm, Lisa saw a pair of black shoes approach and stop just in front of her. Her gaze wandered up to Matt's angry dark face. His blue eyes were like knives as he stared down at her, his mouth twisted in a sneer.

'You dropped this,' he said, holding out a lipstick.

She held out a hand for it.

Adam stood up, drawing her with him. Matt dropped the lipstick into her palm and she slid it into her handbag and snapped the bag shut.

Adam turned away to pay the bill. Matt still stood there, his expression scornful.

'You've had too much to drink,' he said under his breath in a savage voice.

Lisa was armoured against everything tonight. She smiled, her brown eyes shimmering through their lashes at him. 'Not too much,' she said. 'Just enough.'

'What the hell do you think you're playing at?' He was closer now, speaking in an urgent, angry voice. 'What's got into you, Lisa?'

Adam returned, gave Matt a polite withdrawn nod and slid his arm around Lisa. 'Home, Cinderella.'

She let him lead her away without even glancing at Matt. Adam put her into the car and drove away from the restaurant. After a moment he said, 'Our faithful shadow is with us again.'

Lisa had her head snuggled against Adam's shoulder. Sleepily she said, 'Mmm....'

They pulled up outside the block of flats. Adam lifted her out, led her into the lobby and then into the lift. Her eyes half closed, Lisa leaned against him. She felt rather than knew that they had reached the third floor. Adam guided her along the corridor and tapped on the door.

It opened with a snap. Cherry stood there, her eyes sparkling angrily.

'My God!' she breathed, eyeing Lisa. 'Adam, what on earth have you done to her?'

Lisa opened her eyes and smiled at her. 'Hi, Cherry.'

Cherry pulled her through the door with a vengeful hand. Adam moved to follow, but Cherry pushed him away.

'Goodnight, Adam,' she said fiercely. 'I'll talk to you tomorrow—if I ever do again!'

The door slammed shut. Lisa's legs were buckling under her. She sat down on a chair. 'Oh, my head!'

Cherry lifted her with a tug. 'Bed for you, my girl! You can't be let loose on your own, can you? Adam of all people!'

'Adam's sweet,' Lisa said vaguely. 'I love him....'

Cherry gave her a swift, hard look. 'Do you indeed?' She helped her towards the bedroom door, half pulling, half carrying her.

Lisa fell onto the bed, yawning. 'I could sleep for a hundred years.'

'It might be better if you did,' Cherry told her, ruthlessly stripping her.

Lisa rolled over onto the pillow, wearing nothing but the lacy black slip Cherry had lent her. 'Goodnight.'

Cherry snapped off the light and closed the door.

CHAPTER SIX

LISA woke up with a headache and a distinct impression that someone was hammering on her head. After a moment, with a groan, she realised that someone was, indeed, hammering—but on the front door, not her head. Stumbling out of bed, she searched for something to put on and found a filmy pink negligee hanging in the wardrobe. Wrapping it loosely around her, she went to the door. The flat was deserted. Presumably Cherry had gone to work.

She opened the door an inch and peered through the crack. Matt's face appeared.

'Oh!' Vague, unpleasant recollections swamped her. She tried to shut the door again, but Matt kicked it open and pushed past her into the flat.

'You can't come in,' she burbled. 'I'm not dressed. I've just woken up ... oh, Matt, go away ...!' Her voice rose in a wail at the end.

He looked her up and down, his lips contemptuous. 'You look terrible. I suppose you've got one hell of a hangover this morning?'

Her head was throbbing like the motor of a fast car. 'No,' she lied, lifting her chin.

'You little liar,' he said. He glanced round the flat. 'Where's your friend?'

'How did you find me?' She tried to think, but her brain was like cotton wool. 'How did you know this address?'

'Your father gave it to me when I called round and found you'd run away.'

'Run away?' Indignantly she glared at him, her headache suddenly forgotten. 'I'm on holiday. My father suggested it suddenly. It wasn't even my idea.'

'You jumped at it, though, didn't you? You couldn't wait to get away. Have you asked yourself why?'

She knew perfectly well why, but she wasn't going to give him the satisfaction of knowing just how much of an effect he had had on her.

'I haven't had a holiday for years,' she told him coldly. 'I needed new clothes. I've been wanting to come to London to buy some for ages, but I never managed to get away before.'

Again that searing glance ran over her, comprehensively, from her new curls, now tangled and ruffled by sleep, to the lacy negligee she was holding together with one hand.

'Why did you do this to yourself? You've turned yourself into an imitation fashion plate. I liked you the way you were. This sort of sophistication doesn't suit you. You're not the model girl sort, you're a country girl.'

'Who are you to say what sort I am? Mind your own business. Now if you'll excuse me, I must get dressed.' She moved past him to the door, opened it and stood waiting for him to leave.

He moved across the room in a lightning flash, slammed the door shut and caught hold of her shoulders, his fingers biting into her flesh.

'Matt!' she gasped in alarm.

He jerked her towards him so that the negligee fell apart, revealing her slender body in its thin black lace slip. Matt looked down at her hungrily, tracing the whiteness of her breasts, the slim waist.

'Are you trying to drive me out of my mind?' he demanded. 'Last night I had the shock of my life when I saw you. I barely recognised you. Then you drove off with that aged Romeo you've picked up....'

'Adam isn't an aged Romeo! He's charming!'

Matt's face blazed. 'Is he, by God?' His hands instinctively tightened, making her wince, then his face came down towards hers, and she could not stop herself from standing on tiptoe to meet his mouth, her lips parting passionately under his long, hard kiss. His hands slid slowly, lingeringly, along her back under the negligee, warm and caressing. Her blood was rioting along her veins, her heart hammering against her chest. She threw her arms around his neck and surrendered to her desire to touch him, running her fingers down his neck and back.

They were abruptly shaken out of their trance by a sharp rap on the door.

Lisa pushed Matt away, frowning. 'Who on earth?'

Matt looked down at her, breathing heavily, his face dark red. 'I'll see who it is. You'd better get dressed. You look too tempting like that. I might lose my head.'

Going very pink, she rushed into the bathroom and turned on the shower. Stepping under it, she heard voices, masculine voices, raised in cold argument. She frowned. Was Matt having a row with somebody?

Towelling herself rapidly, she slid back into the negligee and went through the door. Matt and Adam were standing in the centre of the sitting-room, glaring at each other like two stags locked in mortal combat.

Adam glanced at her, raised an eyebrow. 'Well, hello again!'

She flushed, realising she was distinctly not dressed for social occasions. 'I'll be back in a minute, Adam,' she said quickly, fleeing to her bedroom.

With fingers that shook she dressed in her dark grey skirt and a white sweater. Brushing her hair, she saw that she looked more like the Lisa she saw in the mirror every day. Only her hair-style remained to remind her of last night's sophistication.

She went out of the bedroom to find Matt standing by the window, his hands thrust into his pockets. He turned at her arrival and looked at her hard.

Adam moved towards her, took one of her hands. 'Ah! So this is what Cinderella looks like in the morning? Are you ready now? We have a date, remember?'

She looked at him blankly. Had they arranged a date for this morning? She had no recollection of it.

'We're going shopping first, then lunch,' Adam told her softly. 'As I was just telling your friend, you won't be free all day.'

She glanced at Matt. He looked at her compellingly.

'I came to take you out myself,' he said, his tone gritty.

'I'm sorry, Matt,' she said slowly. She was tempted to deny that she had a date with Adam, but pride made her change her mind.

Matt's face tightened as if she had struck him.

Adam took her arm. 'Where's your coat?'

She had flung it over a chair when she arrived last night. It still lay there. The flat had been tidied somehow since then. Cherry presumably had done it while she waited for Adam to bring Lisa back.

Adam helped her on with her coat, then turned courteously to Matt.

'Can we give you a lift anywhere?'

'I've got my own car,' Matt snapped.

Adam smiled. 'Then goodbye for now.' He opened the front door and stood aside, obviously inviting Matt to leave. Slowly, reluctantly, Matt walked out. Adam seized Lisa's arm again and ushered her out, too.

Matt walked down the corridor in front of them without saying a word. They waited for a lift in silence, then travelled down in it together.

'How's your head this morning?' Adam asked her teasingly.

'I'm fine,' she lied again.

Matt shot her a nasty look. She ignored it. Adam moved closer, his hand curving round her arm in a possessive gesture which Matt's dangerous blue eyes observed with silent fury.

They left the building and Adam helped her into

his car. Matt walked away without a backward look. Adam drove away into the stream of traffic, whistling under his breath.

Lisa leaned back with a long, anguished sigh.

'Cheer up,' said Adam. 'He'll be back.'

'Who said I wanted him back?' she retorted.

'That's the spirit,' Adam grinned. He gave her a long sidelong glance. 'So what did Cherry say last night?'

'I haven't the foggiest,' she admitted. 'I was past caring. I just fell into bed and went out like a light.'

'Champagne does that to you,' he agreed gravely.

She was forced to laugh. 'Oh, you are the limit! You deliberately set the whole thing up!'

'I think we both needed something of the sort,' he said. 'Cherry has kept me dangling for months. I think she's rather enjoying herself. I let it ride for a while, but I've had enough. I want to marry her, but she'll have to change her way of life, and I don't think she's ready to do that.'

'You want her to give up her job?'

'Not necessarily,' he shook his head. 'All I ask is that she stops rushing around the world. While she was in Tokyo I was lonely. I missed her. Her present job demands that she spend a lot of time out of Britain. No marriage could survive the strain.'

She saw his point. Soberly, she said, 'What if Cherry doesn't agree?'

He shrugged, grimly. 'Then I'll stop seeing her. I can't stand this on-off relationship.'

'Have you actually told her how you feel?'

'Not yet,' said Adam. 'It's been building up inside me for months. Last night I saw red, and I decided to teach her a lesson. If she didn't mind my going off with you, then I've obviously failed.'

'Did she seem annoyed when we got back? I have a vague picture of her being around.'

'She was very cool,' he said thoughtfully. 'But it was hard to tell what she felt. She shut the door in my face.'

'That sounds promising,' Lisa encouraged.

He grinned at her. 'Doesn't it?' He pulled up. 'Ah, a parking space . . . now to do some shopping.'

She blinked at him. 'Were you serious about that?'

'You said last night that it was your main reason for coming to London,' he reminded her.

'Did I? I don't remember.'

'That I can believe,' he grinned. 'I'm surprised you remember anything.'

'Ouch! That isn't kind.'

They walked along a narrow road and emerged into Oxford Street, the busy shopping centre of London, lined with hundreds of shops of all kinds. The autumn sunshine sparkled on plate glass windows and the black tops of taxis. A busker was shuffling along, playing an accordion, the cheerful notes of a popular song wheezing out as he moved.

Adam halted, staring into a window. 'That would suit you,' he told her.

She stared at the warm, orange-russet dress worn by a haughty-looking model. The price made her wince. 'Far too expensive,' she groaned.

'Live dangerously,' Adam urged her.

Firmly she shook her head. 'No. That's much too much.' She walked on and found a shop with dresses within her price range. Adam insisted on coming to help her buy them, waiting outside in the shop while she tried several on in a cubicle. She came out to parade them for him, turning round in front of him.

Adam chose two, in the end. One was a very plain but well-cut dress in a turquoise-greeny shade. The other was lemon yellow, with a deep boat neckline, tight waist and full skirt.

She was astonished by Adam's patience and kindness. He insisted on taking her to buy shoes which would match either dress, and a handbag to match the shoes. They also bought her new lingerie; frilly, expensive and very pretty.

'Aren't you bored?' she asked him.

'I'm enjoying myself,' he insisted. 'It's a pleasure to watch your face. I've never helped a girl choose clothes before, and the novelty of the experience is delightful.'

'What about your work?' she asked. 'I hope you aren't going to lose too much valuable time.'

'Luckily, I'm between cases,' he said, shrugging. 'I should be reading briefs today, but I'll do it tomorrow. I've been working too hard while Cherry was away. I feel like being idle.' His eye was caught by something in a window and he stopped, staring. 'Now that would look great on you,' he told her.

She glanced casually at the short white imitation-fur jacket. 'Can't afford it,' she said.

He pulled her into the shop. Calling over an assistant, he soon had Lisa trying on the jacket. Staring at herself in the mirror, she had to admit she was tempted. It was so warm and luxurious against her skin. 'Oh, I don't know what to do,' she muttered.

'We'll take it,' Adam told the assistant. 'Don't bother to wrap it. She'll wear it.' He handed her Lisa's old coat. 'Put this in a bag, will you?'

Amused, the assistant obeyed. Lisa eyed him fulminatingly. 'It is a ridiculous piece of extravagance,' she told him.

'Good. About time you let yourself be extravagant. Hurry up, I want my lunch. I'm starving.'

Laughing, she paid for the jacket and they left. Adam hailed a taxi and gave an address in St James's.

The restaurant was small, intimate and discreet. They talked while they ate, in their little cubicle, out of sight of the other customers. Adam told her about his work, explaining it crisply and succinctly. Lisa was fascinated, her brown eyes wide with interest. Watching him, she wondered how Cherry could resist him, how she could bear to keep him at arms' length as she obviously had for months. Of course, Cherry had always had no trouble attracting men. She had been spoiled early on in her life, surrounded by eager admirers. No doubt she still had plenty of men eager to take her out. All the same, Adam was something special. If it hadn't been for Matt, Lisa would have fallen for him herself.

At last he leaned back, smiling at her. 'And what are

you going to do about Matt Wolfe?' he asked suddenly, taking her by surprise.

'Do? Nothing.'

He grinned at her hot-cheeked confusion. 'You love him, don't you?'

'I told you, I don't know,' she murmured.

'I do,' Adam said. 'It's obvious.'

She was stricken. 'Do you think Matt knows?' The thought made her feel slightly sick. Remembering the kiss they had exchanged in the flat that morning, she wanted to die. Matt had been kissing her out of a mixture of anger and contempt. She had invited that kiss, throwing herself at him like a wanton. What on earth must Matt think of her now?

'I doubt it,' said Adam, lifting an elegant shoulder in a shrug. 'I'd say his observation isn't too keen.'

She was bewildered. 'What do you mean?'

'Nothing,' Adam said. 'Now look, my dear, you told me all about Livia Marlowe and Matt's desire to keep his mother from knowing that he was going to make a film with her soon. I didn't tell you that I knew Livia.'

'Oh!' She stared at him in consternation. 'She's a friend of yours?'

'An acquaintance,' Adam shrugged. 'But I know her well enough to get an invitation to the party she's giving tonight after appearing in a charity performance in the West End. Will you come with me?'

'I couldn't,' she said, shrinking. The idea of seeing Livia Marlowe, perhaps having to watch her with Matt, made Lisa want to die.

'Of course you could,' Adam insisted. 'Always face the enemy, Lisa. Never run away. Remember, a retreating army is very vulnerable. Matt followed you here when you ran away from Saintpel, didn't he? There's nowhere left to run to.'

She shivered at the words. 'Don't! You're frightening me, Adam.'

He laughed. 'Be careful, Lisa. Are you certain you want to run? I suspect you're very flattered by his persistent pursuit. You're building too much into it. A man like Matt Wolfe doesn't necessarily mean the same thing when he says he's in love as a girl like you may mean. Love is a casual coin in his circle, offered without thought.'

'I know that,' she said faintly. 'That's why I've made it clear to him that I don't want to see him.'

'I wonder if you made it clear enough?' Adam murmured. 'Love makes us all cowards. Are you sure you haven't been giving him the green light without knowing it?'

She thought of the way Matt had kissed her, the confident passion of his arms around her, and her cheeks burned as she remembered her own response again. It wouldn't be surprising if he thought she was giving him the green light. No doubt he interpreted her flight, her angry rejection of him, as mere coyness. He might believe she was deliberately teasing him, leading him on until she finally submitted.

Adam was watching her soberly. 'I'll ring Livia,' he said, after a moment. 'Her party starts at midnight.'

'Midnight?' she repeated in dismay. 'That late?'

'Her charity show ends at eleven-thirty,' Adam explained. 'I'm afraid this sort of party goes on quite late.'

'I've got nothing to wear,' she protested.

'Cherry will find something suitable,' he smiled.

'Cherry?' she repeated, looking at him sideways, her eyes narrowed in a frown. 'Cherry is hardly likely to be very co-operative when she knows I need the dress in order to go out with you again.'

He grinned. 'Leave Cherry to me. It's time I had words with that young woman, anyway.' He rose, paid the bill and guided her out of the restaurant.

In his car he said calmly, 'How would you like to go to a concert tonight?'

She was puzzled. 'A concert? But I thought we were going to this party?'

'Not until eleven-thirty,' he reminded her. 'I have tickets for a Mozart concert at the Royal Festival Hall.'

She looked alarmed. 'Oh, but Adam. . . .'

'Of course, you'll have to go alone,' he broke in, grinning at her understandingly. 'That will give me a chance to talk to Cherry on my own.'

She laughed. 'Oh, I see. Sorry to be so dumb. In that case, thank you.'

He gave her a ticket in a small envelope. 'Hurry back afterwards,' he reminded her. 'Take a taxi.'

She promised to do so and he dropped her at Cherry's flat. She spent the afternoon watching an old film on television, her feet hurting too much for more sightseeing. At six she began to get ready to go to the concert.

When she left the building she stood on the pavement, looking around for a taxi. She had no idea where the Festival Hall was sited.

She saw a taxi throbbing through the busy traffic, its yellow sign declaring that it was for hire, and waved an arm energetically. The taxi swerved over to pick her up, but before it reached her another car drew in beside her and she looked down into Matt's face.

Surprise made her stare at him, her mouth shaping the word, 'Oh!'

'Get in,' he dictated.

Lisa backed, shaking her head.

He opened the door to get her, but the taxi drew up behind him and the driver indignantly put his head out of his window. 'Hey! You all right, miss? He bothering you?'

She fled towards the taxi with Matt staring after her. The driver slammed the door after her, muttering. As they passed Matt he put his head out again and yelled, 'Swine!' at him. Over his shoulder he said to Lisa, 'Men like him make me sick. Pestering strange girls in the street!'

Matt's angry dark face staring after them brought a wild bubble of laughter into her throat, but she suppressed it. She stared out of the taxi window, watching the traffic with curiosity.

Where did all the people come from and where were they all going? They streamed out of offices and shops, heads down, belting along the streets with pale, intent expressions. She wondered what it felt like to work in this huge city among so many other people. Did it make one feel far less of an individual? Or did they get used to the vastness and impersonality and somehow make their own place in this difficult world?

The taxi turned over a bridge and she was able to glimpse the river, glinting silver under the evening sky, its banks lit with soft Victorian lamps which made the light softer than the usual modern ones.

The Festival Hall was lit too, its white modernity softened by the evening. Past it she saw the stark climbing shapes of office blocks which fingered the sky bluntly and were already splotched by squares of yellow light where people were working late into the night.

The taxi stopped to drop her. She hunted through her purse to pay him and smiled as she said goodbye.

'Now you be careful, miss,' he said, noting her soft voice. 'London's full of men like that chap. Always on the make. You have to have your wits about you these days.'

She thanked him and turned to walk into the building. In the crowded foyer she studied a poster advertising the concert, noting that the main attraction was a concerto played by her father's favourite pianist.

How Dad would envy her if he knew she was here! One of his dreams was to be in London and go to a concert every night of the week. Records were a poor substitute for the real thing.

'There you are!' said a furious voice at her elbow.

Lisa turned, her heart leaping, and looked at Matt's dark face incredulously. 'How did you get here?'

'Followed your taxi,' he grunted. 'Damned impudence of that fellow!'

She chuckled, eyeing him teasingly. 'He thought you were trying to pick me up. He warned me about men like you ... men on the make, he called you. Shrewd of him, wasn't it? But then I suppose being a man he recognised what sort of a man you were at a glance.'

His hand gave a dart and seized her wrist, tightening until she gasped with pain and indignation.

'Don't talk to me like that,' he snapped.

She tugged at her wrist. 'You're hurting me!'

'Stand still, then,' he ordered.

She raised angry golden-brown eyes to his face. 'What are you doing, Matt, following me around London?'

'I've got to talk to you,' he said, his eyes intent on her face, making her pulses race with the beauty of their blue brilliance.

Someone gave a little cry nearby. 'Look, Carol, there's Matt Wolfe ... it is Matt Wolfe, isn't it? Imagine seeing him here?'

Matt groaned under his breath.

A large, pink-faced woman pushed a programme under his nose. 'Could you sign this for me, Mr Wolfe? I'm a great admirer of yours. I want this for my daughter. She just loves your series.'

Matt was forced to release Lisa's hand and turn reluctantly, a polite smile on his mouth. While he was signing his name and listening to the woman's out-pourings Lisa darted away into the crowd, moving towards the door by which she would enter the hall.

Matt could not have a ticket and was unlikely to get one at this late stage. Once she was safely in the hall he would not be able to follow her.

Unfortunately there were a large number of people filtering past the ticket collector, and she had to queue up to get inside. She hoped desperately that Matt would be detained long enough to let her escape.

When his hand caught at her shoulder she winced, looking round at him with a pale face.

'I've got to talk to you,' he hissed under his breath.

Aware of the fascinated curiosity of the rest of the queue Lisa felt impelled to let him pull her out of her place and guide her to a quiet corner behind a marble pillar.

He pushed her into the alcove, standing in front of her, his eyes restless on her face.

'You'll make me late for my concert,' she said uneasily, her heart thudding.

'Are you going alone?' he demanded.

She flickered a glance up at his face. 'Why?'

His mouth tightened. 'Skip the concert,' he said in a flat voice. 'Have dinner with me.'

She shook her head. 'No, thank you.'

'Lisa,' his voice burst out, ragged with irritation, 'stop behaving like this.'

'Like what?' she asked innocently. 'I just want to go in and hear that Mozart. Is that so strange? I've been looking forward to it. Wasn't it sweet of Adam to get the tickets?'

'Tickets?' he repeated heavily. 'Do you mean you're going with him? Where is he, then?'

The tail of the queue had disappeared inside the hall. Lisa smiled up at Matt, her eyes cool. 'I'm meeting him later,' she said quietly. 'He can't get here immediately.'

Matt's hand touched hers, his warm fingers caressing. 'Lisa, there's too much to say ... we've got to see each other soon ... when can I see you?'

'I'm rather busy at the moment,' she said lightly. She glanced past him and saw that the hall door was clear. 'I must go,' she said, darting past him.

She heard him coming after her across the marble floor, but she was too quick. As the door swallowed her up Matt arrived there and had to halt. Glancing back, she saw black rage on his handsome face.

CHAPTER SEVEN

LISA got back from the concert, her mind filled with music, to find Adam and Cherry sitting close together on the sofa in a dimly lit room. She did not need any explanations to see what had happened. Their faces said it all. She smiled at them across the room, and Cherry jumped up to run to her, hands outstretched.

'I ought to be angry with you, you little double-crosser,' she said happily. 'But I've decided to forgive you, after all.'

Lisa hugged her. 'I'm glad, so glad!'

'Will you be my bridesmaid? We've been sitting here for hours planning the wedding,' Cherry beamed.

'And other things,' Adam added drily.

Cherry made a face at him. 'Take no notice of him, Lisa. He's above himself tonight.'

'Congratulations, Adam,' Lisa said gently. 'I'm very happy for you both. When is the wedding to be?'

'As soon as possible,' he said. 'I've lost all my patience. Cherry is going to have to make up her mind to it. Her days of freedom are over.'

'What a terrible thought!' said Cherry, her eyes dancing with happiness. She held out a hand to him and he rose to take it, kissing her palm softly. 'Now,' she said, 'go away and come back in an hour to take Lisa to this party. I'll perform another of my transformations. It will take me an hour, I should think.'

Adam left, and Cherry set to work, much as she had done the previous evening. Lisa's mind was full of doubts. What was she doing, letting Cherry dress her like a sophisticated doll? What good would it do? Matt had shown only too clearly how much he despised her. He had told her that she was a country girl, not a sophisticate, and he was right. She was only making a fool of herself. Vulgar curiosity was driving her, curiosity and a burning jealousy of the unknown Livia Marlowe, who had married Matt's friend to spite him and who presumably still loved Matt and wanted to marry him.

When Cherry was finished she pushed Lisa in front of a mirror, and Lisa saw that same tall, slender, enamelled figure she had seen the previous evening.

'You look very good,' Cherry said, without enthusiasm. 'Lisa, are you sure you should go tonight? I'd hate to see you get hurt.'

Lisa glanced at her miserably. 'Adam's told you?'

'About Matt Wolfe? Yes.'

'I wish he hadn't.'

'I was jealous enough to scratch his eyes out if he hadn't,' Cherry said lightly.

'Of course. I'd forgotten.' Lisa smiled wearily at her. 'You had no cause to be jealous, Cherry. Adam's crazy about you. He talked of little else.'

Cherry's eyes lit up. 'Thanks. You must have been a cheery little duo—Adam talking about me, you talking about Matt Wolfe!'

Lisa sighed. 'There's really nothing to talk about. Matt used me as an excuse to his mother.'

'The rat!'

Lisa shrugged. 'I didn't mind that so much, but he shouldn't have kissed me to make it more genuine....'

Cherry eyed her. 'Sure that was the reason he kissed you?'

Lisa nodded grimly. 'Certain. He as good as admitted it. He wanted to be sure I'd play along.'

'He deserves shooting.'

'The trouble is, I can't forget him,' Lisa moaned. 'I'm sure he doesn't care twopence for me, but he's made me love him.' She covered her face with her hands. 'Oh, I was happy enough with Peter until he came along. If I'd married Peter we would have made it work, I expect. It was never going to set the Thames on fire, but we got along very well.'

'Darling, that sounds so dreary!' Cherry said in dismay. 'I'll say this for Matt Wolfe—if he separated you from Peter Farrell he did you a good turn. I'd no idea things were quite so dull between you. You can't marry on the strength of getting along quite well together. It needs more than that to make a marriage work.'

'I suppose you're right,' Lisa sighed. 'All the same, I wish I'd never met Matt.'

'Love can be pretty fatal at times, can't it?' Cherry agreed. 'I know how I felt when I realised you and Adam had gone off together. I felt like death. You'll never know how close I came to killing you last night. I really hated you, Lisa.'

'Don't! You make me feel ashamed,' Lisa confessed in dismay.

'It was all Adam's idea,' Cherry said frankly. 'I'm aware of that. He admitted as much.'

'He wanted to make you jealous.'

'He succeeded!'

Lisa laughed abruptly. 'I told Matt he was despicable for using me to cheat his mother into thinking he wasn't interested in Livia Marlowe. Yet I let Adam use me for similar reasons and it seems to have worked out very well.'

Cherry looked at her compassionately. 'Darling, if you want to get out of this party, I'll cope with Adam.'

Lisa looked at her, tempted. It was a way out, and

she badly wanted to find a way out, yet something held her back from accepting it. Slowly she said, 'Maybe I ought to go. I have to find out how I really feel, how Matt really feels....'

'But you aren't really thinking,' Cherry said swiftly. 'You know how you feel already, and I think it's obvious that Matt Wolfe was just amusing himself down in Saintpel. After all, a man like him must get bored in a small town. He probably wanted to while away the time, and you were to hand. You were almost engaged, which made you just interesting enough. Matt Wolfe would enjoy the challenge of stealing you away from another man. So he turned on the heat, and being the little innocent you are, Lisa, you fell for it.'

Lisa was white. 'You're probably right. At first I thought he was interested in Fran....'

'Oh, Fran would be a pushover for someone like him,' Cherry dismissed easily. 'You were far more of a challenge. His ego would need something more than the fun of making a girl like Fran fall for him.' She looked at Lisa pityingly. 'Darling, forget him. Where's your pride?'

'It's my pride that makes me think I should go,' said Lisa. 'I'm not running away again. Adam said I should face the truth, and I think he's right. I'll go there tonight just to see Matt for the last time. I want to see him with Livia Marlowe. Maybe then I can put him out of my mind. I thought coming to London would help me to forget him, but he followed me here, so it hasn't done the trick. Every time I see him I fall further. I've got to cauterise the wound.'

Cherry shrugged. 'You know yourself best. So long as you aren't fooling yourself.'

'I don't think I am,' Lisa said flatly. 'You don't mind if I borrow Adam for one night?'

'Help yourself,' Cherry said easily. 'I'll sit at home and plan my trousseau.'

Adam arrived a moment or two later and whisked Lisa away, kissing Cherry briefly before they left. In his car he gave Lisa a long, appraising stare.

'You look even more fantastic than you did last night. Cherry is brilliant.'

'I feel like a stranger.'

'Good. That will help you to achieve a sort of distance from what happens. Remember, you have to face the facts, Lisa—whatever the facts turn out to be.'

'I know,' she agreed quietly.

'This is a public performance. Forget Cherry. For tonight I'm your escort. I think you ought to let Matt Wolfe believe I'm interested in you. Don't tell him about Cherry. Let him go on thinking we're dating each other romantically.'

'I hate all this deceit,' she burst out.

'I know, but I think this is necessary. I don't want you to hate yourself tomorrow morning.'

She flushed deeply, remembering the way in which she had risen on tiptoe to meet Matt's kiss. She certainly did not want to betray herself like that again.

Livia Marlowe had an apartment in a modern

block in Chelsea facing the Thames. When they had parked the car they lingered on the Embankment, gazing along the dark water at the reflections of light. The weather had turned colder suddenly. A chill wind blew through the leafless trees, knocking the moored barges together with a dull clang.

'There's the City,' said Adam, pointing back down the river. 'See the dome of St Paul's? And there's the House of Commons.'

Lisa stared, entranced. 'How romantic it all is by lamplight!'

'The lamps along the Embankment are Victorian,' Adam told her. 'They've been kept just as they used to be.'

'They're beautiful,' she sighed. Further down the river they could see a large ship strung with lights which gleamed like will o' the wisps in the darkness.

'Come on,' said Adam, taking her elbow. 'We might as well join the party.'

'Will it be as crowded as the one last night?'

He grinned, shaking his head. 'Not on your life! Livia wouldn't allow it. She likes room to make her entrance.'

The unit was at the very top of a new building. 'The penthouse suite,' said Adam drily as they entered the elevator. 'Must cost a bomb. Livia likes high life.'

The elevator shot up smoothly. Lisa was aware of butterflies in her stomach, but she lifted her chin, determined to face anything that she had to face.

When the doors opened they stepped out onto

When the doors opened they stepped out onto thick, warm blue carpets. The sound of music filtered out to them. Adam leaned on the bell and looked at her, smiling.

'You look fantastic, remember. Whatever you do, keep your cool. I'll do all the talking.'

The door opened and a beautiful blonde girl in a black dress smiled at them.

Livia Marlowe? thought Lisa, smiling back.

'Good evening. Please to come in.' Not Livia Marlowe, Lisa realised. The accent was Swedish.

The girl took their coats and politely indicated the bathroom. Then she led them along the wide, brilliantly lit corridor into an enormous room which seemed very full of people. There was a little silence as they entered. Heads turned, eyes surveyed Lisa comprehensively from head to foot. She saw several eyebrows raised and curious looks exchanged.

A woman turned away from the group of people she was talking to, and gave them a wide, ravishing smile. She was svelte and elegant, her white dress so tight it revealed every part of her supple body, the neckline daringly low so that her small, high breasts were half visible.

Above the purity of her white dress her hair blazed like a fiery beacon. Her eyes were as green as a cat's; slanting, sharp, acquisitive.

She moved towards them, swaying on very high heels, as though she meant to hypnotise every masculine eye with her curved, pliable body.

'Adam!' She breathed his name huskily, as if she had been waiting to see him for hours. 'Lovely to see you.'

She extended a long white hand. Adam bent gracefully to kiss it, and she gave a low, amused laugh. 'Darling, how Gallic! I do adore men who kiss hands.' From beneath her thick, dark lashes she surveyed Lisa with unsmiling curiosity.

'Lisa, this is Livia Marlowe,' Adam said smoothly. 'Lisa has admired you for years, darling. She's so excited to meet you in the flesh.'

Livia gave Lisa a cold smile. 'Really?' She turned back to Adam, her cat's eyes glinting. 'You should use your words more carefully, darling ... in the flesh, indeed! It sounds positively immoral!'

'It's positively enchanting,' he replied with a bland glance which swept her from head to foot. 'Every prospect pleases.'

Livia gave that husky laugh again. 'Flatterer!' She looked past him and her smile seemed to switch on a new heat. 'Excuse me,' she said quickly. 'Lord Cambourne has arrived.'

Adam turned to watch her glide across the room towards a new arrival, her movements even more hypnotic than before. Lord Cambourne turned out to be a tall, thin young man with a thinning hairline and an old/young face with little expression.

Quietly, Adam said to Lisa, 'Lord Cambourne has the advantage of combining a genuine title with a lot of cold business brain. He's a very rich, very eligible young man. Livia will meet her match in him, though, if he does marry her. I doubt if he has a lot of time for sentiment.'

'Perhaps he won't marry her, then,' said Lisa.

Adam looked down at her and smiled. 'You say that as if you hope quite desperately that he will. Want to rescue Matt from her toils?'

'I may just think that any man who married her would have my sympathies,' she said carefully.

'She was rather offhand with you,' he agreed. 'But then she's a man's woman. Other women bore her.'

'Too bad,' Lisa said with a snap.

Adam laughed and surveyed the rest of the guests. They were a well-dressed collection, many of them jewelled and made up expertly. They talked in high, confident voices and sipped their drinks while they stared at each other. A little like dangerous animals wondering who to eat next, Lisa decided with an inward smile.

The Swedish girl materialised, offering them each a drink, her even white teeth flashing in a broad smile. 'There is dancing if you wish,' she said, her eyes on Adam admiringly.

He looked as elegantly distinguished as ever, Lisa thought, looking at him herself. No wonder Cherry was madly in love with him!

Several faces among the crowd stood out—familiar, famous faces who looked bewilderingly unreal in this setting.

All of the guests, however, shared one characteristic with their hostess—they spent most of the time staring around in search of newer, more interesting faces, barely listening to each other, and every now and again they would break away from their group with a bright cry of welcome to embrace or shake hands with a newcomer, only to rapidly grow bored with them, too, and commence that restless, shallow search for someone else once more.

'Let's dance,' said Adam, putting his drink down barely tasted. He led Lisa away to the far end of the long room where the carpet had been rolled back to reveal shining parquet floor on which some guests were dancing to the music which constantly streamed from a stereo outfit hidden somewhere.

Adam pulled her close, his hand holding hers high up close to his shoulder, the other hand sliding round her slender waist. As they moved among the others they were so close she could feel every separate breath he drew. She had never danced with anyone like that before, and it half embarrassed her.

Adam turned his head to smile into her eyes. 'Don't look so worried. Everything has a purpose. Keep smiling at me and don't turn round.'

Her heart leapt against her breastbone. 'He's here?'

'Oh, that look!' Adam groaned. 'Your expression is so sweetly transparent. Yes, he's here. Talking to Livia now.' He moved her round delicately so that she had her back to the other end of the room. Over her shoulder he had a good view of Livia Marlowe and Matt Wolfe. He sighed. Not much doubt about Livia's enthusiasm as she flung her arms around Matt's neck, he thought. He really ought to let Lisa see it, but he had a curious protective desire to shield her from the worst. Maybe Cherry was right—Lisa ought to go home again. Matt Wolfe was dangerous to her.

At that moment Matt casually glanced around the

room. His eyes met Adam's across the whole length of the room. For a split second his face froze. Then the dangerous blue eyes moved on to Lisa's slender, half naked back. Slowly those eyes took in the way Adam was holding her, the lazy intimacy of their bodies moving together so close you could not slide a piece of paper between them. Nothing showed on Matt's face. His expression was almost wooden. Only the cruel blue eyes flickered once, then he turned away.

Yet Adam shivered. Lisa looked up at him wonderingly. 'What's wrong?'

He smiled. 'Nothing. A ghost walking over my grave.' He felt as if he had snatched a wild beast's prey away from under its nose. That brief look from the blue eyes had been like a knife thrust to his ribs.

Deliberately he moved so that Lisa now faced Matt. He felt rather than saw her careful, casual glance down the room, felt the bitter intake of her breath as she saw Matt.

Lord Cambourne was watching expressionlessly as Matt took Livia round the waist, his smile dazzling. They moved away towards the dancing floor, Livia throwing a proprietorial smile backwards at Lord Cambourne, yet clearly in no mind to refuse Matt's request.

Matt took her in his arms with a smoothness which argued long familiarity, and she let her supple body move against his in that exciting, riveting fashion.

Lisa did not mean to watch. She did not want to watch. Yet she could not take her eyes from them. She had to know....

Matt was whispering in Livia's ear, his cheek against hers, his strong brown hand moving against her back intimately.

Livia laughed and lifted her face, and Matt's lips brushed her mouth. The kiss was casual, yet intimate. Lisa felt pain shoot through her, a pain so fierce she almost cried out.

At that instant Matt's eyes moved over Livia's shoulders and met hers.

The blue eyes were narrowed in chilly appraisal. Lisa could not hold his stare. She looked away, aware that her colour was rising, her mouth trembling at the impact of that look.

Adam halted and led her off the floor. 'Another drink now?' he asked.

'Thank you,' she said in a small, lost voice.

He gave her a kind, searching glance. 'Do you want to go? We can easily slip away.'

'No!' Her chin rose defiantly. 'I'll stick it out! I'm not running away.'

'Good girl,' he praised, smiling. He found the Swedish girl, was given two more glasses and handed one to Lisa. Raising his glass, he drank a silent toast to her. She smiled back and drained her glass in a fit of bravado. The champagne she drank yesterday had given her the sort of courage she needed now. Adam's brows rose steeply.

'Hey, hold on! This stuff is lethal to someone with a head as weak as yours!'

'Thank you,' she giggled. The spirit was already

having some effect. She felt warm and sparkling, quite capable of outfacing Matt or Livia Marlowe.

As she glanced around the room she saw Matt and Livia talking to a short, portly man in his late fifties, who was laughing at something Matt had said.

'That's Ralph Tudor, the producer,' Adam told her quietly. 'He's involved in the film they're about to make. A brilliant man, but rather short on tact.'

As Adam spoke the man glanced in their direction and his face lit up with a smile. He waved at Adam, calling to him. 'Well, hi! What are you doing here? Come and join us.'

Adam smiled politely, saying under his breath to Lisa, 'What did I say? No tact.' He put a possessive hand under her arm and guided her over to the little group.

Livia gave him an electric smile, but ignored Lisa. Matt, his hands thrust in his trouser pockets, surveyed them unsmilingly, his black brows level.

'Nice to see you again,' Ralph Tudor said to Adam cheerfully. 'How's tricks?'

'Profitable,' Adam drawled.

Mr Tudor laughed. 'I'll bet!' He looked at Lisa. 'You have a very lovely companion, if I may say so, and I would not say no if you saw fit to introduce us.'

'Lisa, this is Ralph Tudor,' Adam murmured noncommittally.

She smiled shyly, extending her hand. Mr Tudor took hold of it in both his, gazing at her with myopic brown eyes. 'A model? Actress? Which?'

'Neither,' said Adam blandly, before she could answer.

Ralph Tudor's thin brows arched curiously. 'No?' He shot Adam a mischievous smile. 'Or should I be a little discreet here? Is the young lady your ... friend, maybe?'

Lisa felt herself blush. She met Matt's cruel blue stare and looked hurriedly away.

Adam's voice was as cold as ice. 'The young lady is just that, Ralph ... a young lady who works for a living as a doctor's receptionist. Nothing else.'

Ralph Tudor grinned uneasily. 'Sorry if I stood on any toes, chum.' He gave Lisa an apologetic look. 'The error was understandable. You're very lovely, my dear. If you're thinking of breaking into the business I might be able to help you.' Something in the way his brown eyes slid over her made her even more embarrassed.

'Paws down, Rufus,' Matt said sharply. 'The "young lady" is already bespoken, I fancy.'

Adam met his eyes calmly. 'Quite right,' he said softly.

Matt's rapier eyes seemed to grow sharper and brighter at the words. 'Are we to hear marriage bells?'

'I'm certainly thinking along those lines,' answered Adam with a faint, mocking smile.

Matt's lean face darkened. 'Then congratulations are in order,' he said tightly. 'Do we kiss the bride-to-be?'

Lisa, half terrified that he was serious, shrank back against Adam, and at once Matt's eyes noted the movement and lifted to her flushed, anxious face.

Livia did not like so much attention going to another girl. She broke in with a voice like melted icecream. 'How terribly thrilling, Adam darling. But whatever happened to that little Cherry thing you used to run around with?'

Adam shrugged. 'She went off to Tokyo, remember?'

Livia's laughter tinkled like the silver bells on a Christmas tree. 'How silly of her!'

Matt's body was suddenly very still, poised like a spring. 'Cherry thing?' he repeated. He stared commandingly at Lisa. 'I thought you were staying with. . . .'

Adam broke in upon the sentence. 'We really ought to be leaving soon, Livia, but before we go tell me, how are the plans for your film coming along?'

Her green cat's eyes grew brilliant. 'Splendidly, darling,' she breathed. She threaded a hand through Matt's arm. 'Matt has agreed to take the lead, after all. I've got a lucky feeling about this film. It's going to be a big breakthrough for both of us ... world blockbuster, we hope.'

'We damned well know it is,' Ralph Tudor broke in eagerly. 'The plot is great. The characters are great. The writers are great.'

'And the publicity will be phenomenal,' Matt said sardonically. 'Free, too, no doubt.'

Ralph Tudor took the words seriously. 'Sure it'll be free! It's a news story. They'll all want to run something on it.'

Livia snuggled her sleek body against Matt, her hand stroking his hard, muscled chest. 'We'll make sweet music together again, won't we, Matt?'

He looked at her with amused arrogance. 'Don't we always, Livia?'

She practically ate him with her green eyes, her fingers curled against him, the nails delicately scratching at him. 'Mmm ... I can't wait for our big love scenes!'

Matt looked over her head at Lisa. 'Neither can I,' he said sensuously.

Jealousy flared deep inside Lisa like lightning bursting across a dark night sky, consuming what it touched. She could have slapped his handsome, insolent, mocking face. Instead she leant against Adam's arm and looked up at him through her long lashes. 'Mmm ... I'm tired, Adam. Shall we go?'

'Yes, I think we should,' he said at once. 'I have a hell of a lot of work to do tomorrow. Lovely party, Livia. Lovely to see you and hear all about your film, and I wish you all the luck in the world with it.'

Livia smiled at him, her wide, beautiful smile. 'Thank you, angel,' she said.

Adam bent and whispered in her ear. 'Cambourne is looking pretty mad. If I were you I'd soothe him down presently or he may make off with the beautiful Swedish blonde. She's giving him some very alluring smiles.'

Livia's bright smile turned into a tigerish glare. She looked round at Lord Cambourne, who was standing beside the bar, a glass in his hand, talking to the

Swedish girl. 'Oh, is she?' Livia said furiously. 'We'll soon settle her!' She swept away towards the bar, her red hair almost sparkling with rage.

Adam steered Lisa away towards the door. The Swedish girl, her beautiful face crimson, hurried after them to find their coats. She looked as if someone had hissed a gypsy's warning in her ear.

Adam helped Lisa into her coat and turned to take his from the girl. Lisa moved towards the front door, but Matt slid past her and blocked her path. She faced him, her heart thudding inside her like a jungle drumbeat.

The lean, piratical face was expressionless. 'What's all this tomfoolery about, Lisa?' he demanded in a low voice.

She opened her eyes wide. 'What are you talking about?'

'You and the great Q.C. there,' he said in a tone tinged with savagery.

'Adam's a darling, isn't he?' she retorted sweetly.

Matt said something under his breath that sounded remarkably like a swear word. Then Adam was at her side again, taking command of her with a long, powerful arm around her. He gave Matt a nod. 'Goodnight, Wolfe. I should watch Livia. She's playing both ends against the middle, you know.'

'What's that supposed to mean?' Matt asked tautly.

'You and Cambourne,' Adam said coolly. 'She can't marry you both.'

'Who's thinking of marriage?' Matt shrugged.

'There are other, more elastic set-ups.'

'A cosy threesome?' Adam considered the idea. 'Cambourne wouldn't like that.'

Lisa couldn't take any more. She had to get out, get away. She moved towards the door. Matt had to step out of the way. Adam gave him a last nod, then they were outside in the brightly lit corridor. Only when they were in the lift could Lisa relax. Her body sagged against Adam with a painful intake of breath.

'I warned you it wouldn't be pleasant,' he said gently. 'But you had to see. Their world is not the ordinary, warm human world you come from, Lisa. They live in a jungle. They eat each other. Livia has had her hooks into Matt Wolfe for years, and she'd never let him go. But I suspect she may marry Cambourne. That money and his title are very desirable assets to an ambitious girl like Livia, but he isn't exactly sexy, is he? For her kicks I guess she'll still want Matt around, and that situation isn't one you would care to get involved in, you know. It's painful, messy and unpleasant for the innocent passer-by to get involved in their world.'

'She's welcome to him,' she half sobbed.

'That's the attitude! Hate him if you must, but for God's sake, don't fall in love with him.'

'I never wanted to anyway,' she protested. 'I was quite happy when he came down to Saintpel. Why couldn't he leave me alone?'

'There's a streak of cruelty in the man,' said Adam. 'He's ruthlessly egotistic. Actors have to be ego-centred —their whole way of life is one big ego-trip. He gets a kick when he makes a girl fall for him. You were apparently indifferent. So—he turns on the charm and bingo! you fall into his arms. Can't you see what a thrill that must be? Most men are vain, and actors are vainer than the rest.'

'He likes to feel he's irresistible,' she agreed. 'I realised that, of course. I suppose I was stupid enough to hope that....' She broke off. 'Well, I was a fool! I was right the first time. He's just a conceited flirt.'

They drove back to Cherry's flat in silence. She looked at their faces anxiously as she let them in and sighed. 'I see! Was it very bad?'

'I think I'll go to bed,' Lisa said in a quiet voice. 'Goodnight, Adam. Thanks for taking me to the party.'

'Tomorrow we'll all go to see a few of the sights,' he said. 'Cherry? You can get the time off?'

'Why not? It would be fun. We could pretend to be tourists.' They both looked at Lisa invitingly.

'You're very kind, but I think I ought to go home,' she said wearily.

Adam stepped over and lifted her chin. 'Listen to me, Lisa. You aren't going to be a rabbit all your life, are you? You're on holiday and you're going to have a good time. Understand? So—we go out tomorrow and tour the sights?'

She laughed, ashamed of herself. 'Fine. Thanks.'

In bed she lay staring at the dark window, listening to the distant throb of London traffic. She would never get used to that noise in a million years, she decided. It was like the echo of the sea. It went on and on....

Where would they go, tomorrow? There were so many places she wanted to see. Kew Gardens with its Chinese pagoda. Richmond Park and the deer. The City of London with its dozens of famous churches and buildings like the Tower of London and the Monument. She thought about all the places she wanted to visit because it kept her mind from the thought of Matt, but as she drifted into sleep, her barriers dropping as her body weakened, his face flashed into her mind's eye, and she was brought violently to life, her whole body trembling with passion.

Why in God's name had he come to Saintpel? He could have gone anywhere in the wide world. Why had fate chosen that he should visit her quiet, peaceful little part of the world, disturbing her life and ruining her happiness?

CHAPTER EIGHT

FOR the next three days Lisa whirled around London from tourist spot to tourist spot, her camera clicking, her brain vainly trying to take in everything she saw, to imprint it on her memory for ever. She did not expect to be coming back for a long time. These memories would have to last her.

Adam knew his city well. 'I've lived here most of

my life,' he shrugged casually. 'I suppose I know most corners of it.'

'And London has a lot of corners,' Cherry grinned.

'It's vast,' Lisa sighed. 'I had no real conception of how big it was until now. Somehow when you live in the country you conjure up a picture of Trafalgar Square or the Tower of London, and there you are! That's London. But it isn't, is it? London goes on and on ... the little bit of it that the tourists see is only the centre.'

'The heart,' Adam nodded. 'The city goes out in circles, like the ripples on a pond ... Hampstead, Wimbledon, Richmond ... there are villages within the city, villages as big as towns, yet retaining their own individuality. A modern miracle. How long they can go on staying the same, who knows?'

Lisa was feeling tired after her sightseeing. Cherry gave her a sympathetic, careful smile. 'What shall we do tonight?'

They had spent each evening out of the flat without making it too obvious that they were keeping Lisa out of any possible danger of meeting Matt Wolfe again. Somehow Adam had procured tickets for the opera, the ballet, the theatre, in turn.

Lisa was grateful to them but conscious all the time that they were never given the chance to be alone. A newly engaged couple ought to have some time with each other. She yawned blatantly. 'Oh, I'm really so sleepy ... mind if I skip tonight? I really think I should be getting back home tomorrow and I've had so much fun the last few days that I've reached the point of collapse. I would love an early night. But you two must go out. I'll be fine—I'll sleep like the dead.'

They did not have to have their arms twisted. Adam's eyes lit as he looked at Cherry, and she had candles in her eyes, too. They went off hand in hand like children.

Left in the flat alone, Lisa took a long, relaxing bath and went to bed. Drifting off to sleep, she heard the doorbell begin to ring. On the point of getting up to answer it, she suddenly guessed it might be Matt, so she sank down again, pulling the covers over her head.

The ringing went on and on, however. Obviously he had no intention of going away. But how could he know she was in? She groaned. The hall porter! He would have seen Adam and Cherry go out alone. He was a gossiping, curious old man, his main interest in life apparently being that of keeping an eye on the tenants of the flats. Matt would not be above slipping him some money to get information, either.

She could not let Matt go on making that racket. It would disturb the other tenants and give Cherry a bad name.

She slipped into the lacy white negligee Cherry had lent her, and went to the door.

As soon as it began to open Matt shouldered his way through the gap, obviously determined not to give her the chance of closing it with him outside.

Angrily she faced him. 'Why were you making all that noise? People will have gone to bed.'

'At nine o'clock?' His tone was acid. He let his blue eyes travel slowly over her. 'Why turn in so early? Tired?'

'Why else?' She turned away from the probing of his glance, her heart beating so fast it hurt. 'What do you want, Matt? Can't it wait? I need sleep.'

'That isn't all you need,' he said ambiguously. 'Aren't you going to offer me a drink? It's the usual custom on these occasions.'

'This isn't my home,' she said sulkily.

'I doubt if your flatmate would mind,' he retorted in a smooth tone. 'I'll help myself, as you're so inhospitable.'

She turned then, to watch him getting a glass, pouring himself whisky, jetting soda into it. It occurred to her that he was rather paler than usual, his expression tightly under control, as though he was having a problem holding himself back from some violent action. The strong features were taut, the long mouth very straight and unsmiling.

He sauntered to the sofa and flung himself down, the glass in his hand. Sipping the whisky, he surveyed her from beneath dark brows. Lisa felt her nerves tingle.

'What do you want?' she demanded shrilly, trembling. 'Why are you here? Can't you leave me alone?'

'No, I can't,' he told her flatly.

The answer took her breath away. She backed and sat down in a chair as remote from him as possible, sitting straight-backed, staring at him.

When she said nothing his mouth quirked sardonically. 'No comeback? Surely you have something to say, Lisa?'

She dumbly shook her head.

He swallowed a lot of the whisky at once and lowered the glass. Incredibly, she got the feeling that he was nervous and using the drink to fuel his courage. Matt Wolfe nervous? Inwardly she laughed at that scornfully. What a ludicrous idea!

'We started on the wrong foot,' he said suddenly, staring into the amber liquid in his glass. 'I rushed things because I wanted to wake you up to the fact that your long-standing relationship with Peter Farrell was as dead as a doornail. It was obvious to anyone—I saw it at once.'

'From one brief meeting?' Her voice was dry.

'That, and things Fran told me,' he said defensively. 'A love affair which goes on without changing year after year has run out of fuel, Lisa. If you'd loved him you would have been keen to get married. You were stalling. So I deduced that subconsciously you knew damned well you weren't in love, but you didn't know how to get out of it.'

'That was very shrewd of you,' she said quietly.

'I was right,' he flared.

She nodded wearily. 'Yes, you were right. I know now that I don't love Peter. That's all over.'

He gave a sigh. 'Well, I'm glad about that, anyway.' He took another drink of whisky, swirling the liquid around and staring into it afterwards as if trying to decide what to say next.

She stood up. 'Was that all? Having agreed that Peter and I are finished, is there any more to discuss?'

He slammed the glass down and stood up, his lean body violent in motion, striding over to her so quickly she had little time to think before reacting.

As he reached for her she pushed him away, using both hands, her face flushing with anger. 'Don't touch me!'

'Do you honestly think I'm going to stand by and see you ricochet like a lost tennis ball, bouncing off Peter Farrell straight into Adam's arms? I didn't liberate you for him to get the benefit of it....'

'You don't own me!' she flung recklessly.

'Don't I? Maybe I want to,' he retorted, his face dark with anger.

'That's just too bad! I'm a woman, not a toy!'

'I know you're a woman,' he said, his voice suddenly filled with passion.

Her heart forced itself against her breast, beating until she was almost suffocated. Matt was holding her wrists in his powerful grip, bending over her, his eyes piercing her flushed face.

She made herself fight the sweet weakness which was sweeping over her. Her own self-respect demanded it. Glaring up at him, she said scornfully, 'Go back to Livia Marlowe, Matt. She likes playing your sort of games. I don't.'

'You were playing games with Adam Browning at Livia's party,' he said bitterly. 'Enjoyed yourself, didn't you? Dancing so close to him you looked like Siamese twins. What else was that but a deliberate tease?'

She lowered her lashes, knowing he was right. Looking up at him through the thick dark cloud of them, she smiled. 'Maybe I like playing games with Adam.'

'You did it to drive me crazy,' he said furiously.

Her pulses beat deliriously. 'Did I?'

He drew breath harshly. 'You're asking for trouble, do you know that? I'm not famous for my patience.'

'What are you famous for? Apart from living dangerously?' Her tone was deliberately offhand. She did not want to get involved in a three-sided triangle with Livia Marlowe as the third side. When she loved again she meant it to be a man who would love only her. It seemed that Matt had some sort of affair in mind. In a way it was flattering that he should want her, even on such terms, but she did not intend to encourage him. Affairs were all very well in the high-living circles he moved in—the people of Saintpel didn't approve of them.

She tugged at her wrists, trying to free herself. 'Will you let go? You're cutting off my circulation.'

'I'd like to cut off your head,' he said savagely. 'You don't use it much, do you? Try thinking now and then instead of letting your emotions run wild.'

'At least I have emotions,' she flung back. 'All you have is a lust to get your own way!'

He suddenly jerked her wrists so that she fell forward against him. At once his head bent and his mouth sought hers, but she averted her head, shuddering, and his lips fell on her cheek instead and moved slowly, sensuously down the side of her exposed throat. The sensation was exquisite torture. She could not help closing her eyes. The room seemed to be going round and she felt dizzy.

He moved his hands to encircle her, his body hard against her. His face was warm against the coolness of her naked shoulder. She could feel his heart pounding against her. He was breathing fast.

He lifted his head and tried again to kiss her mouth, but she kept her head stiffly averted.

'Why are you pestering me like this?' she made herself ask him coldly. 'Can't you take no for an answer?'

Matt was still for a moment. She felt his body stiffen. 'You've changed,' he said harshly. 'When I first met you, you were sweet and unspoilt, worth ten of your shallow, empty-headed little sister, but since you came to London you seem to have grown hard. You've tried to make yourself sophisticated. Don't you realise you were never meant to be one of these hardboiled London sophisticates? You belong back in Saintpel, not here.'

'I agree,' she said hoarsely. 'I'm going home tomorrow.'

He took her by the shoulders and stared down at her. 'You are?'

She nodded.

'What about Adam Browning?' he demanded.

She laughed. 'Adam? What about him?'

Matt's face worked angrily. 'Don't fence with me, Lisa. At that damned party he said something about wedding bells. Was he just kidding?'

'He meant for him and Cherry,' she said.

Matt stared down at her. 'So she isn't in Tokyo?'

'She's out with Adam now,' Lisa said. She was sick of games. He might as well know the truth.

'And all that dancing cheek to cheek with him was pure makebelieve?'

She nodded. 'I thought it might get you to leave me alone,' she told him frankly.

His face was stiff. 'You thought you needed that sort of protection? You went to some lengths, didn't you? You were behaving like a wanton at that party. You might have given Browning the wrong idea.'

'Adam knew about it,' she said calmly.

'Did Cherry know?'

She nodded.

'I see—a little conspiracy. Charming idea!' He was talking in staccato fashion, his lips tight.

'I told you I didn't want to see you,' she said huskily, 'but you refused to accept it. So we thought we'd dissuade you in another way.'

'You make me sound like the wicked seducer in a melodrama,' he said bitterly. 'God, you must hate me!'

She was silent. Then she said quietly, 'All I want is for you to leave me alone.'

He released her. 'I get the message. Goodnight, Lisa.'

She watched him walk to the door. It closed behind him very quietly. This time she had the feeling she would never see him again, and desolation swept over her in a bitter flood.

She arrived back in Saintpel the following evening looking so different that when her father met her at the station he stared incredulously. 'Is that you? What on earth ...?'

She twirled, laughing, her short silky curls flicking around her face. 'You don't like it?'

'I can't be sure,' he said frankly. 'It'll take a bit of time to get used to it. You certainly look different.'

'I feel different,' she said, her face sobering a little as bitter memories intruded. Then she smiled again, quickly. 'I've spent all the money you gave me, I'm afraid.'

'That's good,' he said firmly. 'You needed new clothes.' He studied her pleated skirt and waist-hugging jacket. 'That's very pretty. Any more like it?'

She patted her suitcase. 'Wait and see! I'm going to make Saintpel sit up!'

They drove back along the quiet, sleepy roads talking easily about events since she left. 'Nothing much has happened,' he said. 'What does happen here? What about London?'

'I saw so many fantastic places,' she said breathlessly. 'I don't know where to start.'

He laughed. 'Sounds as if it was a successful visit.'

She nodded. 'Cherry and her fiancé were very good to me. They showed me their favourite places. I went to the opera, the ballet. ...'

'You certainly seem to have made the most of a few days' holiday,' he agreed, with twinkling eyes. 'You didn't get the itch to stay there, did you?'

'No!' She was certain about that. 'Saintpel is where I belong. London is fine—for a holiday, but I'd hate to live there. For one thing it's hard to get to sleep. The traffic makes such a noise! And it wakes you up again early in the morning, too. I've never seen so many cars. They're terrifying, they seem to choke the roads in all directions.'

He smiled, well satisfied. 'Well, I'm certainly glad to have you back. Fran did her best, but she's a little absentminded. She's totally ruined a couple of saucepans by forgetting she had put something on to cook, and she saturated the potatoes with salt one day...her meals are a bit of a lottery. You never know whether you're going to be able to eat them or not.' He grinned at her. 'Don't breathe a word to her, though. I would hate her to feel she'd failed. She seems quite pleased with her efforts.'

'At least she tried,' Lisa said gently.

'It's half the battle,' he agreed. 'From now on, I shall insist she take over at least one day a week. She can let you have a day off to enjoy yourself. We'd got into a rut, Lisa. You were overworked—Peter was right about that.'

She was quiet for a moment. 'How is Peter?' she asked.

He glanced at her doubtfully. 'Very well,' he replied evasively.

Has he been round while I was away?'

'Now and then,' he admitted.

'Dad, do you think Peter could be attracted to Fran?'

she asked nervously. 'Somehow I got the feeling he might be.'

Doctor Baynard smiled at her gently. 'Would you be very hurt if he was?'

'No,' she said frankly. 'I think Peter and I were never really suited. It was just an old habit.'

'When did you discover this?' he asked shrewdly. 'Before you went away or during your visit to London?'

'I think I've known for a long time, but I began to be sure about it before I went away,' she said.

'Matt Wolfe wouldn't have anything to do with this, would he?' her father asked wryly.

Lisa flushed, her eyes bright and angry. 'Why should you think that?'

'He asked me to give him your address in London,' Doctor Baynard told her. 'Did he look you up?'

'Yes,' she said unrevealingly. 'But he has nothing to do with Peter and me. I don't like him. I don't suppose we'll ever see him again.'

Doctor Baynard's brows lifted quizzically. 'Oh?' He glanced sideways at her pink face. 'I see.' He drew up outside their house. 'As to Peter and Fran,' he said, 'I think I ought to leave you to discover for yourself just how things are.'

Fran came from the kitchen to greet her. 'Lisa! You look terrific!' She walked round her, staring in admiration. 'I never thought you could look so good!'

'Thanks,' Lisa said drily, amused by her sister's bluntness.

'Where did you have your hair styled like that?'

'Cherry did it,' Lisa told her.

Fran's eyes widened in astonishment. 'Cherry! But it's superb!'

'Cherry's very clever,' Lisa agreed. 'I didn't like it at first, but it's grown on me.'

'It's altered your whole appearance,' said Fran. 'Did you get lots of clothes?'

'Quite a few,' Lisa admitted.

'Can I see them?'

'Come up and have a private viewing,' Lisa said teasingly. They went upstairs and she showed Fran her clothes to a chorus of warm admiration and approval. As she hung them in the wardrobe she asked casually, 'Dad says Peter's been round a few times.'

Fran flushed and looked uneasy. 'Er ... yes. He was at a loose end while you were away, so he asked me to go to the cinema one evening. I hope you don't mind?'

Lisa turned and smiled at her. 'To tell you the truth, I couldn't care less.'

'Lisa!' Fran gasped in disbelief. 'What on earth do you mean?'

'Peter and I have been making a mistake,' Lisa said quietly. 'We haven't been in love for years. We just kept on seeing each other because we'd got used to the idea. Once I got away from here I could see that quite clearly. I suspect Peter knows it too, but sooner or later we have to talk about it. Do you think Peter knows, Fran?'

Fran was flushed and excited. 'I ... I think you should ask him that yourself, Lisa. A third party should never interfere in things like that. I might have got

Peter's feelings all wrong and I wouldn't want to hurt either of you.'

Lisa looked at her searchingly, her eyes kind. 'Wouldn't you, Fran? That's sweet of you.' Her little sister seemed to be growing up at last into a thoughtful, responsible woman. Love could work wonders!

Fran looked anxious. 'You do believe me, don't you, Lisa? I'm very fond of you, you know, even if I have seemed rebellious or difficult at times.'

'I understood,' Lisa reassured her. 'Everyone goes through the difficult stage. It's part of growing up.'

Fran's smooth-skinned, delicately featured face broke into a smile. 'You really are a darling!' Because she no longer loved Peter? thought Lisa with amusement. Or because she was understanding?

She saw Peter later that evening. He came into the kitchen, where she was just serving the dinner with Fran, the sisters working in harmony as they moved around the kitchen. Fran seemed more than content to help, Lisa had noticed with pleasure. She had actually insisted on it, in fact. Then Peter arrived, and Lisa saw Fran go scarlet, then white, before she ducked out of the room with a faint confused murmur of excuse.

Peter stood, his hands in his pockets, looking at Lisa in a mixture of astonishment and approval tinged with distant uneasiness.

'Have a nice time, Lisa?' He half moved as if to come and kiss her, then thought better of it and coughed nervously. 'You look lovely.'

'Thank you,' she said blandly, half tempted to be coy

to tease him, then thinking that perhaps she ought to come straight to the point instead. 'Peter, we ought to talk some time.'

His colour rose. 'Oh .., er ... yes ....' He was stammering, quite clearly worried and unsure of himself.

He was afraid she was about to suggest an early marriage date, perhaps, Lisa thought with wry amusement, remembering the number of times he had tried to persuade her to do just that.

Aloud she said, 'Going away has given me a chance to think. Has it ever occurred to you that we might have made a mistake about our feelings for each other?'

He regarded her dazedly, his mouth open. She realised that he could not quite believe what he heard. A sudden qualm struck her. Was she completely wrong after all? Was Peter still in love with her? Was it all imagination that he was really more interested in Fran?

Anxiously, she said, 'I realise it's all a bit sudden, but I suppose being in London gave me a feeling of distance—I could see things more clearly away from home. I don't want to hurt you, Peter. I just want to talk about it honestly and openly.'

'Are you saying. ...' He swallowed. 'Are you saying you don't love me?' His expression was incredulous, but he showed no sign of being deeply hurt. She suspected that he found it hard to believe that any girl could fall out of love with him even if he no longer loved her. Peter had his share of masculine vanity. Matt Wolfe was not the only man to believe himself irresistible.

'Do you mind if I say yes?' she asked him. 'I did love you once, of course, but somehow along the way I think we lost each other.'

Peter was still for a moment, then he relaxed visibly. 'Well, to be frank . . .' he smiled.

'Yes, Peter?' she smiled back sympathetically.

'I was beginning to feel something along those lines myself,' he said clumsily. 'I'm very fond of you, though, Lisa. I guess I always will be. You're . . .' he sought for expression and triumphantly produced the deathless phrase, 'You're more a sister to me than a lover, though.'

Lisa had a hard time stifling a smile. 'I'm glad,' she said quietly. 'I hope we'll always be friends.'

He anxiously searched her face. 'So you won't object if I still come round occasionally?'

'Of course not. I'll be as pleased to see you as I am to see any of our family friends. And I hope you have better luck with your next love.'

Peter flushed. 'Er . . . yes. . . .' Clearly he did not yet feel able to suggest that he might be interested in Fran. He moved to the door. 'I . . . think I'll go and see if Timmy wants any help in laying the table.'

She heard him speaking to Fran a moment later. Their voices sank to a confidential murmur. Lisa went on serving the food with a little smile.

It was going to be lonely for a while. She was going to miss Peter's constant company. Life might be a little grey without any masculine company, but at least she was free to face whatever the future held. She supposed she ought to feel grateful to Matt Wolfe. He had given her a new perspective on life, whatever else he had done. She had been trapped in a stultifying situation and he had freed her. That was something to be grateful for, certainly. If only he had not then gone on to make her fall in love with him instead!

She served the meal and accepted the compliments showered on her with a graceful smile, adding, 'Fran helped a lot. She's learnt to be a really good cook while I was away. I think she's going to be really domesticated.'

Fran grinned. 'Don't get too enthusiastic! I'm not ready to settle down in an apron just yet.'

Peter was watching her closely, his eyes intent. Fran gave him a faint, flickering, provocative glance. He frowned, and Lisa saw Fran's mouth quiver slightly. They were still unsure of each other, she suspected. They were feeling their way in a new, sensitive relationship.

She slept well that night and awoke with a feeling of heaviness which grew into a headache during the morning. After lunch she took Robby for a walk, being careful to keep well away from Storm Dance. The autumn was waning. Cold winds blew in from the sea making the trees toss and bend like dancers. The waves were a steely grey flecked with the white of coming storm. The gulls had flown inland, circling like white flecks over the ploughed earth, their melancholy cries haunting the countryside.

The crisp cold air blew away her headache but did nothing to lighten the ache in her heart.

Nevertheless, the very fact that she was safely home,

in the place she loved more than anywhere else on earth, helped to ease her loneliness over the next few weeks. She found herself falling back into her daily routines without any trouble. She worked hard. It was one way of making sure she had no time to think about Matt Wolfe. If ever she stayed still in one place without occupation she found her mind invaded by him, like a Barbary pirate swarming aboard a Spanish galley. He waited always just beyond the region of rational thought for her mind to lower the barriers she had raised against him, and at the first sign of weakness his dark, cruel face sprang into her thoughts.

There were times when she felt so angry that she could have screamed. There were other times when she merely felt melancholy and depressed. She read the newspapers avidly for some word of him. Stories about his forthcoming film had begun to trickle out. The papers naturally made much of it. There was a lot of mileage to be made out of the background story. Dai Morris's tragic death, Livia Marlowe's involvement with both men, all made it a natural gossip item. Speculation raged about Matt's relationship with Livia. One columnist actually stated outright that she was to marry Matt. At once another, rival, columnist ran a story about her and Lord Cambourne. The public arrival of this peer in the story made a new angle which the papers all pursued hungrily. Pictures of all three appeared. Livia and Matt were both shadowed around London by newshounds and photographers eager for a scoop.

Lisa felt sickened by the whole thing. There was a

ghoulish relish in the way the papers resurrected the story of Dai Morris.

How could Matt bear to be a party to it? He had claimed to be very attached to Dai, yet he was using his terrible death quite unscrupulously to further his acting career. Surely any man with decent civilised instincts would not permit such a personal, searing story to be used like this?

As winter deepened, an army of builders moved into Storm Dance. The gossips of Saintpel made it their business to find out how work was progressing, and the probable date on which the new owner would be moving into the house.

The interior work was finished first because the bad weather made it impossible to do the outside of the house. A constant stream of workmen came and went: plumbers, electricians, plasterers, painters. Matt was apparently sparing no expense.

Christmas was cold that year. There was a promise of snow on Christmas Eve, but somehow it held off, although the leaden sky sagged like a feather bolster over the town and the wind had that bitter nip to it which usually presages snow. The streets were bright with Christmas lights. Outside the church a pine tree was strung with brightly coloured electric bulbs which flashed on and off all night. The shops were crowded. Window displays of toys attracted little knots of excited children. The greengrocers were suddenly redolent of pine and fresh green branches from holly trees, the spicy tang of oranges and the crisp coldness of apples.

As Lisa shopped at the last moment for a few forgotten little things, the local brass band were playing Christmas carols outside the church and the people moved briskly, smiling with that special brightness which magically transforms faces at Christmas.

Walking home, she made a resolution to make this the happiest Christmas ever. She would not once think of Matt Wolfe during the whole holiday. She would be gay and busy, sinking herself in the fun of the season.

'Even if it kills me,' she said aloud, laughing at herself. A neighbour stared in curious amusement, and Lisa grinned at her. 'Good morning! Merry Christmas,' she called across the road, and was given the greeting back.

Her arms full of little parcels, she struggled into the kitchen and sank into a chair. There was so much to do before tomorrow! She liked to get as much of the cooking done on Christmas Eve as she possibly could so that she could enjoy Christmas Day without all the worry of work on her mind. This year Fran had volunteered to help if she could get away, but of course Christmas was as busy a time on the local newspaper as it was at home. There were the usual Christmas stories to pursue and fewer staff to follow them up.

Looking round the kitchen, Lisa sighed and smiled. Although there was so much more work, Christmas brought its own compensation. It was all worthwhile, in the end. For those few days the world seemed to vanish and home seemed an oasis of joy and peace.

CHAPTER NINE

CHRISTMAS DAY was bright and cold. The sun had struggled through the clouds which still hung up there, threatening snow, but the wind was keen as it blew down the narrow, winding streets of the old town and tossed the branches of bare, black trees in the gardens.

After a late breakfast they exchanged their gifts, exclaiming and admiring as they unwrapped perfumes, socks, scarves, books, and all the many personal little items each had chosen. Lisa had bought Timmy a tiny pocket transistor so that he could listen to the radio as he did his paper round in the morning. It had an ear plug attachment so that no one else would be disturbed by the blare of pop music at an unearthly hour. Timmy was enchanted and lapsed into sleepwalking obsession, his ear permanently blocked.

'He'll be deaf by the time he's thirty,' disapproved Doctor Baynard.

Lisa kissed the top of his head. 'All his friends have them, Dad. Timmy wants to be in the swim.'

'You spoil him,' her father grunted, then a smile broke on his face. 'You spoil us all. Thanks for the book, Lisa. I was longing to read it, but the library edition is booked up for months in advance.'

'I saw you mooning over the reviews,' she teased.

'Now you can soak yourself in your favourite subject all Christmas.'

After church they walked back to the house, their cheeks glowing with the wind, exchanging seasonal greetings with everyone they passed. Saintpel was a small place. Everyone knew the doctor's family. They had a special position in local life. It made Lisa feel suddenly happy to be alive, warmed by the warm friendliness of Saintpel.

Lunch was served later than usual, as it was every Christmas, but just in time to sit down with coffee afterwards and listen to the Queen's speech. The sitting-room dripped with gay tinsel and was festooned with swags of red-ribboned holly and ivy, coloured paper chains and frilly Christmas bells. Christmas cards hung in chains from the walls among the holly.

Peter arrived later on and gave them all their presents. He had not distinguished Fran in any way. They all got sensible presents which could be useful in some way. Yet Lisa saw a look pass between her sister and Peter as they exchanged gifts, and the look meant far more than the gifts.

She slipped away to prepare Christmas tea. They always had the same thing—cold turkey sandwiches, jelly and icecream and Christmas cake, solid with icing and marzipan, a fat Father Christmas on top.

Intent on carving the meat, she did not hear the door open behind her, nor was she aware that someone else was in the room until a hand placed a large flat parcel beside her on the table. Then she looked round, surprised and unwary, to have her breath catch with sharp agony as she met Matt's dangerous blue eyes.

'Happy Christmas, Lisa,' he said lightly.

She found it hard to speak. Seeing him was such a pain and pleasure entwined. At last she said huskily, 'What are you doing here?'

'Wishing you a Happy Christmas,' he said, pushing his hands into his pockets. 'I suppose I could have sent my present, but I wanted to give it to you myself.'

She looked at the parcel then, angrily. 'It's very kind of you,' she said in a cold voice, 'but of course I can't accept it.'

'You don't know what it is yet,' he said coolly.

'Whatever it is, I don't want it!'

'Why not, Lisa?' he asked meaningly.

'Because....' her mind stalled, searching desperately for the reasons which had been so clear a moment ago. She turned away sighing. 'Because I can't.'

'At least look at it,' he asked softly.

She looked down at it, unbearably curious to know what he had chosen for her. The shape made it obvious that it was a long-playing record, but which one?

She hesitated, then fumbled with the ribbon tying it, pulling it nervously until the wrappings fell away. Her eyes widened as she saw the name. 'Bach?' It was a surprising choice.

'You remember I played it for you the day you came to Storm Dance?' he asked quietly, watching her face with those intent, disturbing, cruel blue eyes.

She glanced at him and away, suddenly so frightened

her hands were trembling. 'I remember,' she admitted.

'Do you remember what I said then?'

She had no need to search her memory. She thought she could remember every detail of every moment she had spent alone with him. 'You said that the music sounded just the way you wanted Storm Dance to look.'

He nodded. 'I meant more than that, although I couldn't tell you at the time. I thought you were like that music, too. You had a calm, serene face in repose —when you weren't angry with me, that is. You're the Madonna type, Lisa, gentle, peaceful, well balanced.' He looked down at her piercingly. 'Yet you were never that way with me. I wonder why?'

'You're not the peaceful sort,' she said, lifting her chin. 'You're a creature of storm. You blew into our lives and turned everything upside down.'

'Have you sorted things out here? Broken off with Farrell?' His gaze rested on her averted face.

'Yes,' she admitted. 'Not that I have any need to tell you about it. It's my affair.'

'I'm not going to let you go, you know, Lisa,' he said suddenly, his voice soft.

She looked round at him then, her eyes widening, her colour coming and going. 'Let me go? What on earth are you talking about?' She was breathless with anger. 'I've never been yours to keep.'

'You know damned well that's a lie,' he said, suddenly closer, his eyes burning in his face. 'You love me. You may not want to, but you do, all the same.'

Her body was shaken by a sudden violent storm of

feeling. She felt exposed, naked, under his insistent stare. Were her rioting emotions visible on her face? she wondered desperately. Could he tell at a glance of those cruel blue eyes that every pulse in her body was clamouring for the touch of him?

Apparently he could, because with one smooth movement he pulled her into his arms, his mouth possessing her with a hunger that sapped her of all desire to resist, tearing away the barriers she had erected against him, so that a tidal flood of hot passion swept her away with him. For the first time in her life Lisa knew what the desire to surrender meant. A feeling of total abandonment swamped her. She let her hands creep up his shoulders, stroking the hard brown neck, fastening into his black hair. Her skin seemed on fire. Wherever he touched her new pulses leapt into being. The long, cold winter months without him had bred a deep-seated hunger in her which would not now be satisfied.

'Lisa, Lisa,' he groaned, his mouth travelling down her face. 'You're so lovely. I don't know how I've stayed away all this time. I want you. . . .'

She heard a warning voice in her head, a voice she forced herself to listen to reluctantly. Pulling herself away, she looked up at him.

'This is wrong, Matt. Stop it!'

His face was dark red, his eyes brilliant, demanding. 'It's what we both need.'

She could not deny that. Whatever she thought of him as a person, his masculine attraction could not be denied. He only had to touch her to wake fires she had not known existed.

'I'm not a Christmas present,' she said. 'You can't just unwrap me at will. Let me go, Matt. Let me go!' The insistent tone got through to him. He dropped his arms and looked at her stubbornly.

'I shall never go away,' he said slowly. 'I'm a persistent sort of fellow, Lisa. I'll keep battering away at you until you give in, I promise you.'

'I'm not Livia Marlowe,' she cried, wounded and angry. 'I won't be your on-off love even for a few months.'

'My love for ever,' he said soberly. 'I'm crazy about you—you must know that. That first evening when I came back here with Fran and saw you in Farrell's arms, I knew I'd fallen all the way at one glance. You were everything I'd ever wanted, tall and graceful, tender and feminine ... a walking dream. And I was insanely jealous of Farrell before I'd even exchanged a word with him. When you came to Storm Dance next time I started trying to undermine him, getting at you, provoking you. I wanted to wake you up before it was too late. I couldn't let you marry the wrong man.'

'And you're the right one, I suppose?' she asked wryly, not sure how much of all this to believe.

'I know I am,' he said, the bright blue eyes possessive as they ran over her.

'What about Livia?' she demanded, trembling under the battery of his eyes.

'Livia?' He shrugged. 'Once I thought I was in love with her, but that was a long, long time ago. After she married Dai and he was killed, I think I hated her. I blamed her for his death. And I blamed myself. Because she would never have married Dai if I hadn't left her free to amuse herself with him. She only married him to spite me, and once Dai realised she didn't love him he was so miserable he drove like a madman. It was my fault he died.'

'Is that why you gave up racing?' she asked him.

He nodded soberly. 'I suppose so, although I was getting sick of the set-up. It seemed so senseless to risk my life like that day after day. Young men don't mind risking death. I was getting old enough to start caring. I wanted to live. It wasn't so much fear as a sort of irritated common sense.'

'But you kissed Livia at that awful party!' she accused him. 'I saw you!'

'I meant you to,' he said drily. 'I did it for you to see. You know perfectly well that I was jealous of Browning at the time . . . you meant to make me jealous!'

'No,' she denied, flushing. 'I only wanted to make you leave me alone.'

There was a darkness about his eyes as he looked at her. 'Did you honestly believe you could ever get me to leave you alone? I've intended to have you ever since we first met.'

She felt herself shake with answering passion at the hunger in his voice. 'You shouldn't talk to me like that,' she protested weakly.

'I don't want to talk at all,' he said. 'You know what I want to do.'

She forced herself to turn and get on with preparing

the sandwiches. 'I've got to make the tea,' she said huskily.

'When you've got it ready, come out with me,' Matt answered at once. 'I want to show you the new Storm Dance.'

Lisa went on buttering bread, making sandwiches, while he leaned there watching her averted profile, his blue eyes flickering from her mouth to the slight swell of her breasts, down the graceful line of waist, hip and thigh. She could almost feel the hunger in his eyes. Her heart was racing even while her slim hands went on deftly with their work.

Fran came into the kitchen, humming, and stopped dead, seeing Matt. Her curious eyes sped to Lisa's face but got no hint from her sister's calm features.

'Hallo,' she said to Matt. 'I didn't hear you arrive.'

'I came in the back door,' he said quietly.

'Oh?' Again she glanced at Lisa, but her sister went on with her work without a glance. 'I came out to help you,' Fran added.

'Good,' Matt said crisply. 'Because I came to take Lisa out with me. If you take over here, she'll be free to come out.'

'Glad to,' Fran said cheerfully.

Lisa looked round, then, her face confused. She longed to go, yet dreaded being alone with him.

'Get your coat,' Matt said softly, his glance a brilliant blue challenge.

Five minutes later they were in his car driving towards Storm Dance in the fading grey twilight of the afternoon. As they mounted the cliffs the endless rest-lessness of the sea came into view. The horizon was misty. The blood-red orange of the sinking sun left a vivid trail across the pearl-white mist. An oil tanker moved slowly far out to sea, a dramatic black outline as stark as the winter trees.

Matt parked the car in the stable yard and they began to walk around the house. It looked lonely and for-bidding against that desolate sky. Suddenly thin white flakes began flying in the air. The snow had begun to descend at last.

Lisa's eyes brightened. 'Oh, the snow at last! Don't you love it when it snows at Christmas? It only hap-pens once every few years, but when it does it makes such a difference to Christmas!'

'It will get warmer now,' Matt said casually. 'The snow seems to send the temperature back up again.'

They stood outside the great porch watching the snowflakes thicken, whirling in a frantic dance, whip-ped round and round by the icy wind.

'Your hair is turning white,' Matt grinned down at her. 'You look like a snow maiden.'

Lisa put a hand up to brush it away, laughing. Snow melted against her cheek and trickled down inside her collar, making her squirm.

'We'd better go inside,' said Matt. 'You'll catch cold out here.'

'Oh, not yet!' She was like a child in her enjoyment, sticking out her tongue to catch a snowflake and enjoy the sensation of that coldness on her warm tongue.

Matt opened the door and switched on the hall lights. A patina of bright gold fell over the white path. Lisa turned reluctantly and followed him into the house.

He took her coat, shaking it, and hung it up. 'Do you want to take off your shoes, too?' he asked, looking at them.

She glanced down and made a face. 'They're covered with snow, too, I'm afraid. I'd better leave them here.'

The hall looked completely different from the way it had looked when she last came here. It had been painted white and there were thick dark blue carpets everywhere, stretching up the stairs and out of sight.

Matt gestured to her to follow him, and led the way into the room she had found him in before. A transformation had been worked here, too. The delicate apple-green and gold gave the room a new beauty. A fire burnt steadily in the grate. Beside it were some gold brocade chairs, and Matt nodded to one. 'Sit down and get warm. How about a drink?'

Lisa sat down, holding out her frozen hands to the fire. He joined her, offering her a glass of amber liquid that warmed her as it made its way down her throat.

She looked nervously around, admiring the pictures hanging on the walls, the long cushion-piled sofa that matched the chair she sat in, the low coffee table on which lay some open books.

'You're living here already?'

'Temporarily. There are still a lot of things to be done, but they must wait until spring.' He looked at her glass. 'When you've finished that we'll make a tour of inspection.'

She drained her glass and stood up. Matt led her from room to room, pointing out what had been done, smiling when she expressed pleasure. She had to admit he had wrought marvels with the house. He had brought a decaying building back to life. The rooms were still mainly unfurnished, but those which had been fully furnished gave some idea of what the house would look like when it was completely ready for occupation. Matt's taste exactly accorded with her own. None of the rooms was ultra-modern. They were comfortable, homely, yet stylish. Everywhere there was bright, light paint and colourful wallpaper. Storm Dance was still dark and forbidding outside, but inside it was a delightful home.

Back in the living room Matt drew her down onto the sofa. She was immediately nervous again, her face flushing. 'I really ought to go,' she said hastily. 'I must get back home early.'

He shook his head at her, his smile challenging. 'We have all the time in the world.'

She sat upright, her hands on her lap, her eyes restless. 'Matt, please!'

His hand touched one of hers, and the long fingers moved slowly, caressingly, over her skin. She watched like someone in a dream. He lifted her hand very carefully to his mouth, as though she were made of china and might break if he hurried. His lips moved against her palm, her wrist, sensuous and unhurried.

He slid his arm around her and leaned back against the sofa, pulling her back with him. Her head fell against his shoulder and she could not bring herself to move away. The firelight flickered over them. Matt's hand moved away, reached up to a cord and suddenly the room was dark except for the orange glow of the fire.

Alarm flashed inside her. She began to struggle up, but he was holding her too tightly now.

'You're like a wild bird,' he whispered. 'You fly into a panic every time I touch you.'

'Please let me go,' she gasped, aware of a burning desire pounding in her veins, terrified by her own response to him. She just did not know how to handle her own feelings. He terrified and elated her. She wanted to sink back into his arms and surrender—and at the same time she wanted to run and keep on running until he was far away from her. He was too attractive, too dangerous, too sure of himself.

'Don't be frightened,' he whispered. 'I'm not going to go too fast for you this time, my darling. I'll be as gentle as a lamb.' His mouth moved closer to her ear, brushing it, then began to slide along her chin, touching the corner of her mouth. With a faint gasp of awakened sensuality she turned her head to meet his lips. The expected onslaught did not happen, however. Gently, softly, he kissed her, then his lips were gone.

Lisa was bewildered, doubtful, watching his dark face closely. He brushed back a wisp of her chestnut hair, his fingers stroking insidiously along the oval of her face, discovering the angle of the cheekbones, the nose, the parted softness of the lips.

Half dreamily, lulled by his slow caresses, she lifted a hand to touch his hair and face, learning the shape of his head, the hard arrogant features yielding their secrets to the touch of her finger tips.

Matt leant forward slowly, his eyes on her parted lips. She closed her eyes before his mouth touched her, and her hands pulled his head down, her body suddenly consumed with the need to feel him nearer.

The slow, experimental kiss deepened and grew hot. His body moved, crushing her back against the piled cushions so that she slid down among them, her limbs lethargic with pleasure, her whole body curved in response. She could hear her own heart beating until it deafened her. All rational thought was suspended under the impact of the rushing waters of sweet oblivion. She clung to him helplessly, giving back kiss for kiss, feeling the hardness of him against the whole length of her body so that she grew more and more dazed and submissive.

His hands were touching her hungrily, closing over the curve of her hard breasts, running over her restlessly. His lips followed in turn, burning down into the white hollow between the breasts, leaving a smouldering trail of passion where they touched.

When he raised himself to look down at her she was flushed and feverish with desire, her half closed eyes alight with passion.

'I love you,' he said hoarsely. 'You drive me mad—

God knows why. I've seen far more beautiful women and they left me cold. But you only have to turn your head and I feel my body leap into flame. I can hardly keep my hands off you.' She could feel the hard, restless urgency in his body as he spoke. His muscles were tense, his eyes brilliant with desire. 'I want to marry you, Lisa,' he said in a low voice. 'I want to have you for ever.'

For a moment she did not move, her eyes still watching him from beneath their drooping lids, her hair tumbled around her hot face.

She raised her hand and pushed back his dark hair tenderly. 'You may get tired of me,' she said quietly.

His burning glance devoured her. 'Never. You're not the sort of woman a man tires of, darling. You're the sort he builds a home for, as I have here at Storm Dance, the sort he wants for a mother to his children, the sort he wants so much it hurts. . . .' He smiled half wearily. 'You've already put me through all the tortures of hell, Lisa. Put me out of my misery. I couldn't be more yours if I tried. Say you'll marry me.'

'If I refuse?' she asked, half teasing, half serious.

His face grew dangerously menacing. 'I won't let you. I'll keep you here a prisoner until you say yes.'

She laughed, her eyes opening wide. 'Barbarian! You wouldn't dare!'

He bent and kissed her hard, his mouth bruising in its demands. 'Say yes, damn you!' He kissed her again, wringing a response, forcing her to kiss him back. 'Say yes!'

Gasping, her temperature rising again, she said 'Yes,' and began to laugh as she saw the relief, the delight, on his face.

'Are you making fun of me?' he demanded, his mouth wry. His dark face descended again, the blue eyes cruel and ruthless, the mouth compelling her lips to part for him. Lisa moaned softly, her arms locked around his neck, yearning to give herself entirely to him now. The thought of waiting was unbearable.

Suddenly he stopped. His face was suffused with a hard, hot flush, his eyes burnt with a deep glow. 'I'm hungry,' he said harshly. 'Will you get us a meal?'

She stared at him in astonishment, broken out of her dream. 'You want to eat?' It seemed unbelievable that he did not want what she wanted, the total, drowning abandonment of thought.

'Darling,' he said with a groan, 'if we stay here like this for another moment I'm going to lose my head. I think we should do something sane and sensible like eating supper.'

She looked at him through her lashes, smiling provocatively. 'I never expected you to be so down to earth.'

'I'm not down to earth, Lisa,' he said drily. 'I'm floating way up in the stratosphere without a parachute.'

'It sounds dangerous,' she laughed. 'Oddly enough I feel the same. Could it be catching?'

Matt looked down at her, his cruel mouth softened into incredible tenderness. 'Come on, darling. Think how shocked my mother would be to know how close I came to anticipating the wedding ceremony! I'll have something simple to eat. I'm not really hungry at all, but it will occupy our minds less dangerously for a while until my temperature goes down.'

'Perhaps it would be safer,' she agreed, with another brief glance. Her eyes warmed. 'There's just one thing I must tell you first.'

He looked at her warily. 'Yes?' She saw him tensed for another struggle with her qualms of doubt.

She lifted his hand to her cheek. 'I love you.'

Matt caught his breath. 'Lisa, my darling!'

She laughed and moved away. 'Come now, we said supper,' she teased, leaving the room.

For a moment Matt stared after her, his expression urgent with passion, then he followed her and closed the door. The firelight flickered over the quiet, serene room and outside the white snow fell thickly, carpeting the cliffs with a delicate crystalline purity under a winter moon.

Great old favorites...
Harlequin Classic Library
Complete and mail this coupon today!

Harlequin Reader Service

In U.S.A.
MPO Box 707
Niagara Falls, N.Y. 14302

In Canada
649 Ontario St.
Stratford, Ontario, N5A 6W2

Please send me the following novels from the Harlequin Classic Library.
I am enclosing my check or money order for $1.25 for each novel ordered,
plus 59¢ to cover postage and handling. If I order all nine titles at one time,
I will receive a free book, *The Shorn Lamb*, by Lucy Agnes Hancock.

☐ 19	☐ 22	☐ 25
☐ 20	☐ 23	☐ 26
☐ 21	☐ 24	☐ 27

Number of novels checked @ $1.25 each = $ _____

N.Y. State residents add appropriate sales tax $ _____

Postage and handling $ _____ .5__

                                         TOTAL $ _____

I enclose _____
(Please send check or money order. We cannot be responsible for cash sent
through the mail.)
Prices subject to change without notice.

Name _____
                    (Please Print)

Address _____

City _____

State/Prov. _____

Zip/Postal Code _____

Offer expires April 30, 1981.   0105631X

HARLEQUIN CLASSIC LIBRARY

Great old romance classics from our
early publishing lists.

On the following page is a coupon with which
you may order any or all of these titles. If you
order all nine at one time, you will receive a free
book—*The Shorn Lamb*, a heartwarming classic
romance by Lucy Agnes Hancock.

The third set of nine novels in the
HARLEQUIN CLASSIC LIBRARY